Collette's Foot

Pamela Lamb

Agneau Press
2010

First published August 2010 by Agneau Press
Email: agneaupress@optusnet.com.au

ISBN 978-0-9580489-6-5

Edited by: Sandi Jones
Cover design from an original photograph
taken by the author at Noosa, May 2010

For
David

ONE

Collette Flowers walked down the hill through the long grass, disturbing small insects that jumped and whirred ahead of her. It was still misty in the steep valley below the house but she could see the trees on the far slope, thick and green, and beyond, the stark grey shape of Mount Startle looming up into the hot pale sky. The shed, with its rusty iron roof and grey unpainted walls, was tucked into a corner of the steep field, next to a stone wall and sheltered by a huge mango tree. The big nanny goat stood with her back to the door, her legs spread apart to accommodate her pink freckled udder. Collette's mother Nina sat on an upended log, her head pressed against the goat's flank. Balanced on the uneven floor was an old metal bucket half full of frothy milk.

Collette went into the shed and looked down at her mother. Nina's hair was smooth and glossy, twisted up on top of her head and held in place with a plastic comb.

'You're in my light.'

'Sorry.' Collette moved. 'I just came to tell you I was on my way.'

Nina stopped milking and looked up. 'I won't come and see you off. I've got to start the yoghurt after I've done this. It's market day on Friday.'

'I'll see you, then.'

'Let me know how you get on.'

Nina turned back to the goat.

Fleur, the old brindled bitch, who had been sleeping in a flea-ridden dirt patch between the roots of the mango tree, got up when Collette came out of the shed, shook herself,

1

and followed the girl as she toiled back up the hill. It was a ten minute walk from the house to the gate and Collette and Fleur trudged it together, walking down the track and through dusty paddocks where they disturbed a flock of galahs feeding amongst the old seed heads. They crossed the sluggish, half-dry creek by the log bridge and came finally to the edge of the farm, where the thin grey road looped itself around the hillside. There was a wooden platform by the gate where the milk churns had stood in the days when there were cows to be milked. Collette and the dog heaved themselves up and sat side by side on the soft, warm timber.

It was eight o'clock in the morning and already hot.

Five minutes later the bus came staggering around the corner with a full load of kids on their way to school in Ney Creek, the small town beyond the valley. It stopped with a spurt of gravel to let Collette climb aboard. The old dog stood and watched the bus until it was out of sight, then she turned and walked slowly home.

'Where'ya goin', Cauliflower?' A big boy, his face red with pimples, leered at Collette.

'There's a seat next to me,' said another boy, standing up with mock politeness. 'You can sit by the window, if you like.'

'What's in the bag, Cauliflower? You going somewhere?'

Collette grabbed her bag and shoved it between her feet. She was standing in the narrow aisle between the rows of seats, a small, plump girl with pale hair and a round, freckled face. The bus lurched and swayed, driving at speed along the narrow country road, and she was having trouble staying on her feet.

'I'm not going to school,' she said. 'That's one thing for sure.'

'Not going to school?' said the red-faced boy. 'Oooh! Tell the teacher!'

'I don't have to,' she said, standing alone in the aisle with the faces staring. 'I was fifteen last week. So I don't have to go to school any more. Don't have to look at your ugly faces. So suck on that.'

2

The bus drove over the new concrete bridge on the outskirts of town and came to a halt in the main street. All the kids got off and went across the street into the snack bar, leaving their bags in an untidy heap on the footpath. Mr. Jackson, the bus driver, climbed out of the bus and lit a smoke. Collette stood next to him, her bag at her feet.

He squinted at her through the smoke from his cigarette. 'Where'ya off to, young lady?'

'You're going to Black Rock today, aren't you?'

'It's Wednesday.'

'That's where I wanna go.'

'You'll have Mrs Parkinson for company. She always goes to the Rock on Wednesdays.'

'Oh, shit. Does she?'

'Why d'you think I'm having this before I get back in?' He pulled the half-smoked cigarette out of his mouth and stared at it reflectively. 'What're you going to the Rock for anyway?'

'I'm just going there. I don't have to go to school any more. I'm fifteen ...'

'Yeah, yeah, I heard.'

The bus driver took two more greedy puffs before grinding the cigarette under his heel and reaching in his pocket for another. 'But what are you going to do when you get there?'

'I might not stay there. There are plenty of other places I can go.'

The bus driver grinned. 'S'pose you're right.' He squinted up the street, the new cigarette stuck in the corner of his mouth while he searched his pockets for a match. 'Doesn't look like Mrs Parkinson's coming. Must be my lucky day.' He picked up Collette's bag and swung himself into the bus.

It was an hour's journey from Ney Creek to Black Rock, an hour spent following the narrow bitumen road down the valley, picking up people from farm gates and small settlements until, by the time they reached the coast, the bus was full of women with small children and shopping baskets, and sounding like a chook-pen at sunrise. Collette spent the whole journey on the back seat, where the big boys sat, and ended up sharing it with two old women in polyester frocks and sensible shoes who sat, legs spread out comfortably under their shiny floral skirts, discussing an unknown young woman with a depth and thoroughness that left Collette breathless.

By the time it reached the sea, Ney Creek had become Ney River, flowing swift and deep between thick stands of mangroves before emptying itself between high rock walls into the Tasman Sea. The town of Black Rock was perched on the coast between the Ney River estuary and the huge monolith jutting out into the sea to the south: the black rock itself which gave the town its name.

The town was popular with surfers who rode the waves on either side of the Rock, depending on the direction of the wind, and with hang-gliders and model plane enthusiasts who threw either themselves or their models off the Rock in search of their own particular thrill. There was a caravan park and a boat-hire shop by the river, and a couple of motels along the sea front. The normal jumble of shops followed the main street steeply climbing towards the Rock.

Mr Jackson pulled up in the middle of town. He shut off the engine and climbed out. He lit a cigarette and watched through eyes half-shut against the glare as the blue smoke from his cigarette chased the black smoke from the bus exhaust which, blown by the stiff breeze from the sea, was uncurling its noxious tendrils across the street.

'Here we are then,' he said to Collette. 'There's a backpackers up the hill ...' nodding with his head, '... or you might be able to get yourself an on site 'van in the park. Okay, then?'

Collette, who only wanted him to go away so that she could start feeling as if she had truly left home, nodded briefly and bent to pick up her bag.

'I'll be back on Friday.' Mr Jackson grinned at her through the smoke. 'Just in case you want to go back home.'

Collette turned her back on the bus driver and began walking in the direction of the Rock. It took her half an hour to climb to the top where the wind was strong and cold, plucking at her clothes. She bathed her face under a tap and sat down on the short, rabbit-nibbled turf. In front of her was the great expanse of ocean like a bright moving carpet spread out to the horizon where a ship lay suspended in the heat dazzle. She opened her bag and pulled out a cloth-wrapped parcel containing several hunks of home-made bread, some soft goat's cheese and a handful of small red tomatoes. She checked that her money was still there - almost eighty dollars in mixed notes and coins. It had taken her six months to get such an amount, stolen little by little from her mother's cash tin every week after the Friday market. Now it represented the difference between success and an ignominious return home with the grinning Mr Jackson. After her meal she lay down and slept while the sun shifted slowly in the sky until the shadows from a small copse of trees crept out to cover her body and she woke up, suddenly cold.

The Black Rock caravan park occupied a flat, sprawling area of land between the town and the river. One side faced the ocean, protected from the tide by a high wall of jumbled rocks. On the river side there was a narrow strip of damp sand where the children played and men cleaned their fish in the afternoons. Tin boats were drawn up on the coarse grass where miserable palm trees rattled their fronds in the strong, salt-laden wind. Here, too, were several unkempt brick barbeques and a set of rusty swings over which small children fought constantly. Collette's caravan was in the tightly packed row that ran from the amenities block down to the river. It was sheltered by a large tree that dropped green nuts onto the caravan roof.

For Collette, who lived on market-bought vegetables and home-made yoghurt, the unemployment benefit, or job-search allowance as it was somewhat whimsically called, was more than enough to live on. Indeed it was a source of constant amazement that it was always there every fortnight when Collette visited the bank and would remain so in exchange for a rather desultory attempt to look for work in a town where there clearly wasn't any. And the caravan, with its musty canvas annexe and the patch of mould on the ceiling above a mattress that had never been dry in its life, represented freedom in its most exquisite sense. The only thing she lacked was a TV. But that would have been luxury indeed.

It had been the woman from social services who had introduced her to the possibility of such delights. She had visited Collette's school one day the previous winter. Standing in front of a class of restless teenagers she had begun to speak in a language as dry as the dust from the playing field outside the classroom window, which was being scooped up and blown about by a strong, cold wind. But, after a while, Collette had begun to pay attention. It seemed that, once she turned fifteen, she would be able to leave school and, hence, be paid by the government to do nothing at all. In fact, according to this woman, it was her right and privilege to claim this money, plus generous allowances for medical expenses and transport, which would enable her to lead the sort of life that should be within the grasp of all Australians whether they were able to find work or not.

It was a powerful message.

By November the weather had turned hot and the town was full. Old cars laden with surf boards lined the beach front. Young families occupied the motels and wandered the hot streets, laden with beach umbrellas and bags full of swimming gear. Nappies jostled with T-shirts and board shorts on the caravan park washing lines.

Returning from the beach one afternoon, Collette found a red sports car crammed into the space between her caravan and the one next door. The next-door caravan had all its windows open and the sides of the annexe were flipped up over the roof to reveal a jumble of sports bags and surf boards tossed down on the concrete floor. A carton of beer with a bottle of rum shoved neck down amongst the bottles stood by the open caravan door. The sound of young male laughter floated out from the open windows of the caravan, mingled with the smell of fish and chips. It seemed she had neighbours.

She met one of them later when she took her bucket full of dirty dishes up to the laundry. He was sitting on one of the wooden ironing boards, eyes half-closed against the smoke of his cigarette, reading one of the scruffy magazines from the damp cardboard box that lay under the big table in the middle of the room. Next to him the washing machine rumbled. He was about eighteen, tall and lean with pale brown curly hair tied in a pony-tail. A silver ring shone in one ear. He looked up and grinned. 'Got any pegs I can borrow? We came away in a bit of a hurry. '

Collette dumped her bucket on the draining board of the nearest sink.

'I'll get them in a minute. Your washing's not finished yet.'

The boy hopped down off the ironing board and held out his hand.

'Name's Terry.'

'I think you're next door to me. In that red car.'

Terry grinned. 'It's not mine, unfortunately. Come on, we'll go and get your pegs and I'll introduce you to Michael.'

Terry's friend was stretched out on an air mattress laid out on the annexe floor in the middle of the chaos. His eyes were shut. His arms folded behind his head. His feet crossed comfortably at the ankle. He was not pleased to be woken. He was not impressed by Collette, a small, dumpy girl with a twist of coloured cloth around her body. Dark eyes surveyed her from the bed. He managed a, 'How ya going?' then closed his eyes again. He hadn't bothered to change his position. Collette thought he was better looking than Terry. Tanned skin. Brown hair, cropped short. Even lying down, Collette could see the muscles in his chest and arms.

She went into her own caravan and fetched her pegs which were in a bag shaped like an old-fashioned apron and hung on a coat hanger, something she had bought from a market stall in a fit of home-making zeal just after she moved in. Collette and Terry washed Collette's dishes while they waited for the washing machine to finish, then they hung the wet clothes on one of the washing lines, standing together in the narrow gap between other people's towels while the mosquitoes zinged and stung

Back at the caravan, Terry reached in to the fridge, extracted two stubbies of beer, twisted their caps off and handed one to Collette. Michael was still on the mattress, fully asleep, turned on his side with his hands tucked into his arm-pits.

'What's up with him?'

Terry shrugged 'He's always the same when we come away. Something to do with his dad. He gives him a hard time.'

They were walking along the gravel road towards the river.

'Who gives who a hard time? Him or his father?'

Terry grinned. 'Bit of both, I think. Still, I wouldn't mind having a dad like that.' He jerked his thumb over his shoulder. 'He bought him that car for a start.'

They sat on the grass with their backs against the trunk of one of the palm trees. In front of them the river rolled energetically towards the sea.

Collette put the neck of the beer bottle between her teeth and drank. She was surprised by the sharp, cold taste of the beer and how much she liked it.

'Smoke?'

She shook her head.

Terry lit his cigarette and inhaled deeply. 'I shouldn't, I know. They're so fucking expensive.' He looked down at the pale dish of the girl's face. 'I don't have a rich daddy like Michael. I've got to work for a living.'

'You should go on the dole.'

But Terry shook his head. 'I'm a full-time student. And I can't get Austudy. Dad's got too much money for that. He owns a newsagency.' He pulled a face. 'That's where I've got to work after Christmas.' He blew out a lungful of smoke. 'Still, that's the way it goes. A month's holiday then two months' work and then back to uni.'

'What about him? Michael?'

'His dad gives him an allowance. So he can stay away for the whole of the vacation.'

'So. What'll he do?'

Terry shrugged. 'Depends on the surf. He might go south. He's got people in Sydney.' He flicked the remains of his smoke and watched the speck of light arch away. 'Though he probably won't. He says he will every year but he never does. It's his mum, see? In Sydney. I don't think he's seen her since he was a little kid.'

8

The only thing Michael liked about Collette was her yoghurt. It was his habit to drink heavily every night and then go out surfing early in the morning and he discovered that Collette's yoghurt had an immediate and lasting effect on his hangover. However, he found it too bitter to eat unsweetened, as she did, so each evening while the new batch of yoghurt was fermenting in a cracked enamel bowl on Collette's draining board, he and Collette would go out searching for mango trees with ripe fruit to steal.

Collette didn't think of it as stealing. Her childhood had contained few of the things money can buy but there had always been an abundance of fruit: mangoes, watermelons, bananas and small, sweet tomatoes. In her opinion, ripe mangoes belonged as much to her as to the flying foxes that plundered them nightly, never mind that they were growing in somebody else's yard. Michael enjoyed the stealing for its own sake and for the sake of the warm, sweet fruit shoved anyhow into his mouth on the way home. Often they walked back along the beach and swam in the cool, limpid water, tracked in silver by the rising moon. They seldom spoke.

For Collette, already half-way in love with him, the best part of these expeditions was the shock of his touch when he piled their haul of fruit into the cradle of her arms. It never occurred to her that he touched her breasts deliberately.

TWO

In the last week of November the council decorated the pine trees in the beach-front park with coloured lights which swayed in the stiff afternoon breeze, occasionally clashing against each other and showering the ground with shards of glass. The tops of the street lights were hung with green and red tinsel so that the pelicans that roosted there looked as if they were sitting on shiny, exotic nests.

One afternoon Collette came home clutching a watermelon, undecided whether to swim first or take herself off with the melon and a sharp knife to sit in the shade and watch the river. On her way into the park she glanced at the notice board outside the manager's office.

'There's a message for you,' she said to Michael who swore vigorously and stumped off towards the office.

'What's wrong with him this time?' Collette carried the melon into the boys' caravan and hunted in the drawer for a knife. 'D'you want some of this?'

Terry was sitting at the table with his laptop open in front of him. He looked up and smiled. 'Please.'

'What's wrong with Michael?' she repeated as she began hacking at the melon.

'Results are out.'

'Did he fail?'

'Nah. Did well, as always.'

'How about you?'

A grin 'Failed one. But I knew I would. I'm doing IT, see? And I've got to pass programming. I've failed it once already. Just as well they'll give me another go next year.'

'What's IT?'

Holding two chunks of dripping melon Collette wriggled her way onto the upholstered bench behind the table.

'Information technology. You know. Computers.'

'Oh, yeah, I know about them.'

Which piece of information, strangely enough, was perfectly true. The town of Ney Creek where Collette had gone to school, although inhabited almost exclusively by ex-hippies and impoverished farmers, had the advantage of being right in the middle of the most marginal seat in the state. At the last election, the Labor party had wrested it from the Nationals by a margin so narrow that it had taken two weeks for the poll to be declared. Six months later, along with low-interest loans for the farmers and job-start programs for the hippies, the local high school had found itself at the receiving end of a truck-load of computers, delivered with the compliments of the Education Minister.

One of them was installed at the back of the Year 12 classroom for the use of the couple of bright kids in the school and the misuse of everyone else who played games on it in the lunch hour and quickly infected it with a variety of viruses brought in on pirated discs. The rest of them were put into an empty demountable building next to the football field and loaded with word-processing packages and spreadsheets. The girls took to them like ducks to water, their heads full of the fancy jobs they would be able to get in a bank or a real estate office.

So Collette, surprising though it may seem, knew about computers. And liked them too. There was something very agreeable about that blank, shiny screen and the little blinking square waiting patiently for her to tell it what to do. It was a lot nicer than Nancy, the goat at home, who kicked Collette whenever she got the chance, or the wood stove in the kitchen that always went out whenever there were cakes to bake or Collette wanted hot water to wash her hair.

Michael stood one-legged on the hot concrete floor of the phone box and wished he'd taken the time to put on his shoes. The girl on the other end was another in the long line of good-looking females with whom his father liked to surround himself. She had a high-pitched voice and spoke of Michael's father as if she owned him. Which she very well might do, thought Michael, or at least for the time being.

After an amount of time calculated to remind Michael just who was who in the relationship and during which Michael considered, and rejected, the thought of hanging up, he heard his father's voice. Urbane, charming and friendly, as it always was, it had its customary effect on Michael, that of driving him to the brink of tears. It was congratulations that his father was offering and a mild query regarding the result in one of his four subjects which was not quite up to Michael's usual standard. Michael's reply was taciturn, just short of being rude, while he bit down on the surge of anger that threatened to overwhelm him.

'Will we see you at Christmas? Naomi has great things planned.'

'I dunno. I'll let you know.'

The beeps went.

'Okay, Dad. I've got to go.'

When Michael got back to the caravan, Terry and Collette were sitting very close together staring at the screen of Terry's laptop computer.

Michael ignored them. He opened the fridge and pulled out a bottle of beer. He threw himself down on the bed at the other end of the 'van, propped his head up on one folded arm and drained the bottle.

'Make us a curry tonight, Collette, eh?'

Terry raised his eye-brows at Collette. 'Wanna swim?'

Despite the young girl's obvious preference for his friend, a natural hazard for anyone who chose to be friends with someone as attractive as Michael O'Shea, Terry still nursed the hope that he and Collette might get together before his holiday was over. For someone used to a regular and varied sex life, even if most of the girls he got with were Michael's cast-offs or the friends of Michael's girls, Terry had lived a curiously monastic life since his arrival in Black Rock. Michael had devoted himself to the bottle and the sea, purging himself of whatever it was that was keeping him self-absorbed and short-tempered. They had kept away from the pubs and Michael hadn't even bothered chatting up the checkout chicks in the supermarket, however hard the girls competed for his attention whenever the two boys went in to stock up on boxes of Weet-bix and lumps of steak which was their staple diet.

Terry and Collette had spent a far bit of time together while Michael drank or slept off the effects and Terry had discovered that Collette's company had an unexpected charm. She was not given to talking, made wonderful food out of very little, did their washing up with her own and acquiesced willingly to any request or demand he made of her. If he wanted to go swimming, they swam. If he wanted to go to the bottle shop in Michael's car, she sat peacefully in the passenger seat and stared around her. If he wanted to sit by the river and drink beer, they drank beer and she trotted happily to and from the caravan with fresh supplies. But he soon discovered Collette was not tuned in to the subtleties of sexual advances, especially sexual advances Terry-style which lacked the dynamite effect of Michael's technique. But Collette had sat very close to him while they looked at his computer and he had felt her leg warm against his and she had not moved when he put his foot on top of hers.

Terry and Collette stayed at the beach until it was dark and the sea was warmer than the breeze. At sunset the dolphins came in close to the shore and swam with them. Then they sat on the beach, wrapped in their towels, and watched the first star appear in the evening sky. Terry put his arm around Collette and kissed her. He felt her body respond, her weight shifting until she was resting against him, her mouth upturned to his. He pushed her gently onto her back and unfastened the towel around her chest. He felt her shiver. Her old faded togs clung to her body. He tugged at the narrow straps over her shoulder and he felt her wriggle herself out of them. He peeled the damp sticky nylon from her breasts and watched them move heavily. They were large, pale, pink-tipped, patterned with blue veins. Salty to the taste. He felt himself rise. Harden. Three weeks of celibacy made the anticipation sweeter, the wait harder to bear. Resting on one elbow, his hand caressed between her thighs. But Collette struggled. She sat up and tugged at her togs.

'Come on, let's go home.'

'What for?'

'I've got to cook Michael a curry.'

Michael woke at two o'clock in the morning. He was lying awkwardly on the air mattress in the annexe of his caravan. It was hot and stuffy. His neck ached and he had a raging thirst. He went into the caravan for a drink of water. Another need arose. He got as far as a scruffy garden bed at the end of the path where he urinated on an old geranium plant, legs straddled, staring up at the night sky, heavy with stars.

Michael had no recollection of the musty-smelling curtain that hung just inside the door to the annexe. But he was in no mood to work out where it had come from. He stumbled on until he was free of its embrace and then fell heavily onto the mattress. That a girl was there surprised him only a little. He had no memory of the previous night's events. In fact, everything that had happened to him since he'd spoken to his father that afternoon had faded into a sort of jumbled video-tape in his mind with the image of a technicoloured vegetable curry recurring a few too many times for comfort.

It was several nights since Collette had dragged her mattress into the annexe. The caravan was too hot and she preferred the mosquitoes to the hordes of cockroaches that tap-danced across her bed every night and the rifle-shots of the small green nuts falling on the roof above her head. When Michael lifted up the sheet and crawled in beside her Collette was dead asleep. She sighed and moved over, making room. She was used to sharing her bed. When she was a little kid she had slept in the bunkhouse with the other children. Most of the time there were more children than beds. While the adults talked and laughed and made music in the big house, the children ran around in the dark until they dropped with exhaustion and then crawled into whatever space they could find.

14

It was seven o'clock when Michael woke again and looked around him. The green canvas roof above his head glowed with the hot light of morning, the moving branches of the tree outside creating random black shadows. The remains of a mosquito coil stood on the floor, grey smoke curling, reminding him of holidays long gone. He had moved in the night and had ended up taking up more than his fair share of the bed. Collette lay crammed up against the canvas wall, but she was still sleeping peacefully.

He studied her thoughtfully. Asleep, she looked like a child. Her skin smelled of warm soap, her breath, faintly, of the beer she had drunk last night. She was wearing a large white T-shirt. Nothing else. He had no recollection of having sex with her, which was unusual for him. But then he had been unusually drunk last night. It was strange that he had woken up feeling so good.

He lay on his back and tried to remember what had happened. He remembered sitting at Collette's table drinking beer and watching her cook. Then - ah, yes! - the curry fiery and hot in his gullet. Then later, sitting by the river in the dark. He remembered wanting to throw himself into the water, an urge he must have resisted because here he was in a dry bed. Looking up at the stars. He remembered doing that. He had his penis in his hand at that point, but what he doing with it was anybody's guess.

She was not his type. That was for sure. He never slept with the ugly ones. Never had to. But here she was in his bed. Something must have happened. How strange that he couldn't remember what. For Michael sex was never just sex. He liked it to be more than that. After all, it was what he did best. Or so he told himself. He enjoyed music with it, opera in particular - Mozart he loved, or Puccini's impossibly romantic arias - but it didn't really matter what it was so long as it had those wonderful mellow tenor voices and a love duet with a soaring soprano. Other times he would turn on the radio and listen to that. Or the telly. Lie on the floor and let the coloured light flicker on bare skin and listen to the canned laughter on some second-hand show while he got on with something worth doing. Because it could all get very boring and pedestrian, if you let it, and Michael had a very low boredom threshold. That was half his trouble. More than half his trouble, if the truth was known.

He put his hand out and touched Collette's breast.

Her eyes flew open. 'Hey! What d'you think you're doing?'

'You're in my bed. I just thought …'

'This is my bed.'

'Is it?'

Michael turned his head. A breeze had started up, stirring the lengths of coloured material hanging from the roof. He could see now that they were beach wraps, sarongs, the things girls wrapped around their bodies after they had been swimming. They gave the annexe an exotic appearance. He turned back to Collette.

'Did anything happen last night?'

'You got drunk and puked up my curry. That's what happened. In the bushes,' she added, as if he had asked the question.

'I'm sorry.'

Michael was confused. Somehow Collette had gained the upper hand and he didn't like it much.

'Collette …'

'No, Michael, nothing happened last night. And nothing's gonna happen this morning neither.' Collette climbed to her feet and balanced on the lumpy mattress, staring down at him. 'I'm off for a pee, then I'm going swimming.'

When Collette had stumped off with a threadbare towel and her stringy old togs over her shoulder, Michael lay with his hands behind his head watching the sarongs twisting in the warm air. He grinned. Later, then.

After lunch Michael and Collette went into town. Michael parked his car in the main street and extracted a large number of fifty dollar notes from the teller machine outside the bank. He stood for a moment with the money in his hand then stowed it carefully into a battered cloth wallet that he pulled out of the back pocket of his shorts. And with that gesture it seemed as if whatever had been eating him all the time he had been in Black Rock suddenly stopped biting

He took Collette into the surf shop on the corner and told her to buy herself a new pair of togs. While she struggled in the change room he sprawled on a chair and watched the young sales girls failing over themselves in an effort to please him. Finally Collette chose a navy blue one-piece decorated with white sea-shells and at the last minute he pulled another off the pile that one of the assistants was taking to hang up. It was swirled in bright pink, lemon and aquamarine and would make Collette look like a pale ghost, the reason she had rejected it.

'Not both!' said Collette, coming breathless from the change room in time to see Michael peeling fifties from his wallet and laying them on the counter.

'Why not? You wear them all the time. And you can throw that old one away when we get home. You won't need it any more.'

With the expensive-looking bag tossed onto the back seat of the car, Michael drove to the pub for lunch. The one he favoured was not the red-brick monstrosity in the main street but the Railway Bar a little way out of town. It was a remnant of the days when there was a branch line into Black Rock and a fine wooden railway station with a waiting room where the ladies could sit away from the dust and soot that dirtied their dresses, and a bar where the beers were lined up three deep on the counter ready for the daily swill - ten minutes to drink as much as you could while the engine took on water and the parcels were unloaded. The wall between the bar and the ladies' waiting room had been knocked down to create a long, narrow room. Big double doors opened onto what was left of the platform and a fine view of the dusty banksia scrub and the new shopping centre beyond.

The Railway Bar was where the townspeople went to drink, away from the hurly-burly of the town pub which was full of the sound of poker machines and young men shouting. The Railway was a rough pub at night, especially at the week-end when the live bands were on and the local lads turned up for a fight. In the late afternoons the road gangs came in to sink a few beers and buy a six-pack to take home. But, at lunch time, it was quiet. The local real estate agent was there most days, parking his Mercedes outside, and drinking a quiet beer at the bar while he stared wistfully at all the land that didn't have a For Sale sign on it. There were two old blokes who walked up to the shopping centre a couple of times a week to pick up bits and pieces for their wives and called in on their way home, dropping their plastic bags of groceries under the table, and sitting over a beer while their wives gave up on them and ate their lunch alone.

Out on the platform Michael nodded a greeting to another of the lunch-time regulars, a tall, rangy man with thick greying hair who was sitting at a table at the end of the platform with his back to a lush pink bougainvillea growing on a trellis. He was drinking beer and whisky chasers, his table crowded with empty glasses.

'That's Frank Duncan,' said Michael ushering Collette to a seat. 'You know. He used to be Inspector Darbyshire on TV.'

And then, in response to Collette's blank face. 'Come on, Collette! Where've you been?'

Frank waved a half-empty beer glass at them, 'Lovely day.' He half-stood, remembering some long-forgotten social graces, and touched his hand to an invisible hat.

Michael ordered steaks.

'You don't eat enough meat,' he said to Collette, plonking the laden plate in front of her. 'Look how pale you are.'

They drank beer and Michael accepted a whisky from Frank, who came over to their table.

'It'll be good fishing tonight,' he said to Michael. 'The moon's full.'

The old man lived in a shack on the other side of the Rock and made his living painting beach scenes which were sold in a little gift shop upstream from the town where the highway crossed the river.

When they got home they found Terry outside the caravan with one of the girls from Woollies. They were sitting on brand-new folding chairs.

'They were on special,' Terry explained. 'Fourteen ninety-nine each.'

'Twelve dollars,' said the girl

'Oh, yes, I forgot. Tania gave me discount.'

Terry reached under his chair and dragged out a plastic esky with a blue lid. 'Stops me having to go into the caravan all the time,' he said, handing Michael a beer. 'I got to save my energy, haven't I, Tania?'

Tania giggled.

That evening the four of them squashed into Michael's car and drove to the next town where there was a seafood restaurant supplied by the fishing fleet based in the river. Several more of Michael's fifties were spent on a platter of prawns, crabs and oysters, washed down with bottles of cold white wine bought from the pub across the street.

When they got home, Michael dragged Collette's mattress out of her annexe and replaced it with his own airbed. His large portable CD player was installed on a chair with its power cord going into the caravan through the nearest window. Collette was treated to Michael at his very best, accompanied by the love duet from Madam Butterfly. She thought it sounded like cats. But she enjoyed Michael.

THREE

On Christmas Eve Terry caught the last bus out of town, a bus that would land him in Brisbane in the late afternoon with enough time to do his Christmas shopping before he found a pub with some mates in it and eventually made his way home. He had managed to forgive Michael for hijacking Collette, shaken him by the hand and, sitting in a window seat in the half-empty bus, regarded them almost benevolently as they stood arm in arm on the hot footpath waving him off. After all, Collette hadn't been much to write home about and she certainly wasn't worth a fight between old mates. The odd thing was that he had never seen Michael looking so relaxed

With Christmas over and the town in full swing for the rest of the holiday season, Michael and Collette decided to do a little sight-seeing. The first day they took a cooked chook and a watermelon and went into the hills, Michael driving fast along narrow, winding roads until they came to a patch of rainforest and a swift-flowing creek. Collette had brought a blanket and they lay in the damp shade, listening to the rush of the water and the cicadas loud in the trees.

Michael took off Collette's shirt and succeeded in dousing her breasts with champagne, having poured a sufficient quantity down her throat beforehand that she was unable to object. The champagne made Collette giggle, which was something entirely new, and then become sleepy which was less of a surprise, Collette slept often and suddenly, a habit that irritated Michael profoundly

'You lived around here somewhere, didn't you?' said Michael on the way home.

20

They had driven past the gate to the old farm on the way up but Collette had said nothing. There had been a magpie on the wooden platform where the milk churns used to sit. She'd heard its song as they drove by.

'Tell me about it.' Michael said, his hands firm on the wheel, glancing at her as the car went through a tunnel of shade patterned with patches of bright sunlight.

'Tell you what?' Collette was still a little dizzy from the champagne. The warm air blew through the car window, buffetting her head

'About where you used to live. Come on, Collette I want to know.'

'There's not much to tell. It's just a bit of dirt. Only me and Mum there when I left. I used to help with the yoghurt and the cheese. Mum makes them for the Friday markets in Ney Creek. And I looked after the chooks and the vegetable garden. I had to cart water from the creek in the dry weather to water the plants. Just as well we get plenty of rain up here.'

'Sounds like hard work.'

'It wasn't like that all the time.'

The car came out of the trees onto a high, wind-swept ridge with the sea glittering on the horizon beyond the green distances. The afternoon sun threw hot light through the windscreen. Collette closed her eyes.

It was a long time since she had thought about home. But now she found she couldn't help it. And it was not the home she had left behind that she thought of, run-down and depressing as it was, but the home of her childhood when it had been full of life. Roger and Jenny. They turned up out of the blue one day with a new born baby slung on Roger's back. Four more children were born at regular intervals, each one an exact replica of the one before. Roger was an inventor. He installed the irrigation system for the vegetable garden, worked by an old bicycle. He wanted to harness kid-power, there being an abundance of it on the farm, but the kids always managed to be somewhere else when there was any pedalling to do. Jenny kept coloured sheep in the front paddock. She spun their wool into yarn, then knitted it into lumpy jumpers which everyone tried to avoid wearing. Most nights it was Jenny who cooked the evening meal. Standing by the wood stove, hand in the small of her back, children at her feet while she stirred the big black pot full of rice and vegetables.

Then there was John, the wheat farmer from Western Australia. His wife had died of cancer and John blamed the chemicals he'd used on the farm. Having spent most of his life growing vast acres of a single crop, he'd become interested in biodiversity. He kept up a lively correspondence with a group of people in America who collected the seeds of old varieties of vegetables no longer grown by commercial farmers. It was one of John's sons who had introduced Collette to the joys of sex, taking her around the back of the bunk house and kissing her violently while he plunged his hand into her shorts with frantic haste.

That was the family. The everyday people who lived there all the time. Sometimes there were more. In the summer they would come, pledging their lives to the community, only to leave when the cold winds began to whistle through the canvas covering the kitchen window and the water in the makeshift shower by the back door sent icy needles onto their skin.

Then there was Cliff. Always Cliff. Well named, he was. Sitting at the head of the table, a great rock of a man, with his bushy grey-streaked beard and his big hands that he laid flat on the table while he spoke. It was Cliff who had started the community. Named it Hill End. It was supposed to be the end of care, living there. The end of the rainbow. For him, it was. While everyone left, one by one, to continue their lives elsewhere, Cliff stayed. He would never leave.

But then he died. A year ago now. They said it was a heart attack. He had gone down the slope below the cave that lay beneath the old goat shed, chasing after Nancy's kid which had wandered off. Nina had found him, face down, and had driven the old ute five miles down the road to the telephone. Where he was, they couldn't get an ambulance to him and he was a big man to carry up the slope and all that distance to the road so they had brought a helicopter in, hovering above the thick trees while they winched him up, strapped onto a flat board that turned slowly around and around as it rose into the air.

Michael glanced at Collette, who seemed to have fallen into one of her sudden sleeps, and shrugged. Concentrating on his driving, he had forgotten what they had been talking about. He turned the car into the narrow road that led down the mountain in a series of sharp curves and sudden bends and settled down to enjoy himself.

For the next couple of days, wind and tide combined to make good surf and they spent their mornings at the beach, Collette, wrapped in a towel, reading or sleeping while Michael went out looking for waves. Towards noon when the sand was shimmering with heat and Michael was tired of hanging around in the line-up with try-hard tourists and little kids with their Christmas boogie boards, they went up to the Railway for lunch, often spending the afternoon sitting on the veranda in the oppressive heat drinking with Frank and the old blokes who told them about their war days spent in New Guinea, forgetting as they did so that Michael and Collette were too young even to remember Vietnam

Hadn't been born, or at least Collette hadn't. But Michael had come into the world on the very last day of that war, his mother having gone into labour on the day the Americans evacuated Saigon. She had sat in her hospital bed watching television pictures of people scrambling over the iron gates of the embassy and passing their children into helicopters waiting on the embassy lawn, and of the helicopters shoved off the aircraft carriers into the sea to make room for more. An extraordinary day but one which Michael remembered not at all.

By the middle of the week the beach was no good. The wind was blowing the wrong way and chopping up the waves. They drove over the Rock to have a look at the beach on the other side - a long wide beach, empty except for blowing sand and a big black dog chasing gulls. They walked along the water's edge, searching for Frank's house, and finally discovered it tucked into the dunes a little way back from the beach. It was crouched under a rusted tin roof, surrounded by a gone-mad garden, and, if it had not been for the sunlight glinting on a pane of glass, they would not have seen it at all. They went back to the car and Michael drove through town and along the river, looking for the place that sold Frank's paintings.

'If they're any good, I'll buy you one,' he said to Collette.

They found it eventually, a pretty wooden building sitting almost under the bridge that carried the highway over the river. The river was wider here and there were oyster leases on the other side; narrow wooden walkways between poles standing in the river mud and wire baskets in between where the oysters grew. Tied to one of the posts was a tin boat, with a long-necked black bird standing on the prow. Beyond the river bank the land rose steeply, the slope covered with thick rainforest loud with insects.

Michael parked the car and they sat on a wide veranda overlooking the river, set with wooden tables and chairs and big glazed pots planted with flowering shrubs. The man who came out to serve them was small and quick. He was almost bald, with his remaining hair brushed into a pale fuzz. He provided toasted sandwiches, served in baskets, and enormous iced coffees. He asked if he could tempt them with fresh scones, just a few, left over from morning tea. These, too, came in a basket, wrapped in a starched white napkin. Butter and jam in pottery jars.

'Not bad.' Michael stretched himself out in his chair and watched the river through half-closed eyes.

After lunch they went into the little gallery which was cool and pleasant after the sun outside.

They saw Frank's paintings, which neither of them liked, then spent time browsing a collection of wooden bowls and pottery. From a display of silver jewellery in a glass case Michael bought Collette a pair of ear-rings - dolphins hanging from silver wires. Collette looked puzzled when he handed them to her in a white paper bag.

'I don't have any holes in my ears.'

'We'll do it this afternoon,' said Michael, looking at her fondly.

The following week, as if to herald the end of summer, the weather changed. A cyclone came racketing down from the tropics and hovered just off-shore. The sky was covered with thick, grey clouds. The wind settled down to a steady blow, knocking the pelicans off their perches and throwing handfuls of rain horizontally into the town. Holiday-makers packed up and went home. Those that were left in the caravan park secured their vans with heavy rope and metal pegs, tied their tin boats to trees and got the beer in. There would be no fishing for a while.

In a welter of spray and foam the waves rolled around the Rock and roared up the narrow strip of sand into the little park, engulfing the play equipment and tearing out chunks of grass. In the shifting murk men ran along the beach, through the maelstrom of water, heads bent against the cold sting of wind-driven spray. They were carrying surfboards. Their wetsuits streaming with water, they entered the wild sea one by one at the place where a stream of out-flowing water, littered with lumps of vegetation, would carry them beyond the breakers. For a surfer, to ride the waves created by a cyclone is the ultimate thrill. And, for once, they had the waves to themselves. The dolphins, having more sense, had retreated off-shore.

Collette, who seldom told people what to do nor even expressed an opinion, watched Michael go with a sick dread then walked up to the laundry to do some washing. She had a headache throbbing relentlessly behind her eyes. Her ears were sore and swollen where Michael had pierced them with a darning needle sterilized in the flame of the gas stove. Etched on her mind was an image of Michael out in the madness of the ocean.

A few hours later he turned up, shivering with cold and excitement. It was pouring with rain, the water streaming from an iron-grey sky. He found Collette in the laundry drinking beer with the some of the old blokes who had filled one of the sinks with ice and tall brown bottles. He padded across the room and took Collette in his arms, nuzzling his face into her hair.

'Don't worry. I won't be going out again. Plenty of things to do on dry land that are better than that. Anyway, I broke my board.'

FOUR

And then it was February.

When Michael left Black Rock to return to university he didn't know that Collette was pregnant. Neither did Collette. The child, newly arrived and busy making itself comfortable in the rich lining of Collette's womb, had not as yet made its presence felt. But, even if Michael had known, it would have made no difference to what he did. His father's generosity depended on one thing - that he attend university and pass his exams. He didn't find it too difficult. He had failed to get into law by the narrowest margin and was doing some sort of business course. He hadn't wanted to do law in the first place - it had been his father's ambition, not his - and the only advantage of the course he was doing was that he could pass the exams with the minimum of effort.

The assignments he handled in his own way. He slept with the bright girls, to pinch their ideas, and then slept with the dumb ones to get the work typed up and spell-checked. These latter happy girls gained not only a night of love with Michael O'Shea but also access to some wonderful material which they poached unscrupulously. The result was that once-original ideas made their way AIDS-like through the department. The lecturers could never manage to work out what was happening and tended to mark down the clever girls on the basis that their ideas were obviously not as original as they seemed and mark up the dumb ones for knowing more than they had given them credit for. As for Michael, what we would all expect to happen, even in the 90s, the so-called age of equality, did indeed happen. He got the best marks of all.

When Michael was eight years old, his mother Raelene, who had been attending aerobic classes in the hope of regaining both her figure and her husband's wavering attention, ran away with her gym instructor who not only admired her newly-trim figure and the feisty look in her eye but anticipated the large amount of money she would receive as a divorce settlement.

Raelene, the gym instructor - a man with a finely-tuned body and a foul temper - Michael and his younger sister went to Sydney and settled in a rented flat in an outer suburb while they waited for the large sums of money to start arriving. After six weeks, Raelene sent Michael home. He was a trouble-maker, she said. He was causing conflict between her and her new partner. Besides which, he had eczema, nasty red flaky patches all over his body and he scratched constantly. If she wanted something that scratched, she'd buy a dog.

Michael's father had lost no time forming a liaison with Naomi Halliday, a young solicitor in his practice. She was a gorgeous creature with alabaster skin and thick, auburn hair, the kind of red-head that makes the ordinary, freckly sort wish they were dead. Or she was. John O'Shea saw his new love as a consummate career woman. She was bright and ambitious and he looked forward to having her as his wife and taking her on his arm into galleries and theatres, or picking her up from her city office to have dinner together in a favourite BYO. The sort of thing they had been doing already for quite some time, usually ending with sex in her flash Riverside apartment and a hasty car-ride home late at night.

But as soon as Naomi was settled in John's house, she began nest-building. She dismantled Raelene's smart decor and replaced it with the casual-country look she favoured. Laura Ashley curtains. Lots of cushions on large upholstered armchairs. A scrubbed pine hutch in the dining room, full of Italian crockery and dried flowers. She gave up her job in the city, and the junior partnership that was to have been hers by the end of the year, and took an office in the local shopping centre, doing the kind of everyday law that she had previously despised. But, despite her fondness for home-cooked casseroles and crusty bread from the bakery, she was not impressed by the arrival of a small, angry boy with patchy red skin and a look in his eyes that made her feel more than a little uncomfortable. She told John so, in bed that night and Michael was sent off to boarding school without delay.

It is a popular belief that you can make a problem go away by throwing money at it. There was no doubt that Michael was a problem. And by the simple act of writing a large cheque every quarter, the boy effectively disappeared. John found he could manage to forget about his son most of the time, while his new wife proceeded to fill up his house with pretty little babies of her own.

Michael O'Shea was just the sort of boy that school masters hate. He had that uncanny knack of discovering their weaknesses and then he played on them unmercifully. And how could the unfortunate teacher, subjected to such treatment, go to the headmaster and say, he makes me look a fool? He invented all sorts of ways of creating mayhem in the boarding house, the discipline of which was mostly in the hands of senior boys, but it was other boys who got caught red-handed for the various stupid and sometimes dangerous things that went on, while Michael watched from the side-lines.

After a while, those in charge came to recognise Michael's hand - as unmistakeable as a serial killer's signature for those in the know - in the complaints brought to them by irate masters and seniors biting back tears but what could they do? John O'Shea was an old boy of the school and a generous benefactor. Besides, it looked like he was breeding up a new set of sons who would undoubtedly want places in some school or other in the years to come.

And Michael was clever. How it must have annoyed them! Besides having a quick intelligence, he applied himself diligently to his studies After all, it was either that or sport and he had no time for sport. Or, at least, not for the sort of sport they played at school. Shoving his head up some sweaty idiot's backside in order to gain possession of a ball that was then going to be removed from him in a way that was inevitably painful was not his idea of a Saturday afternoon's entertainment. Even if there were girls with blond hair and Country Road sweaters to chat up afterwards.

By the time Michael's senior year arrived, Australia was in the grip of a recession and youth unemployment was at an all time high. Places at university were eagerly sought and, despite his teachers' predictions, Michael missed out on a place in Law School. He enjoyed the look of disappointment on his father's face and settled down to a business course that would qualify him eventually to become a dickhead in a dark suit doing something useless in the city. He didn't really care. So long as he had his car and money in his pocket so that he could meet girls and go surfing he didn't care. But it was hard work leaving Collette, that's for sure. Probably the most, difficult thing he'd ever had to do.

It was the middle of February when Collette got up one morning and went straight to the toilet to be sick. And it didn't take her very long to work out what was going on. Living a life in which clocks and calendars played no part, she had never taken much notice of her periods which had started when she was twelve and had come and gone regularly ever since. But, sitting on the toilet floor, still too shaky to get up, she realised quite quickly that she had not had a period since Christmas. And that was more than six weeks ago.

Michael had been gone for two weeks. Had left her with the remains of his broken surf board, a fridge full of cold beer and the scent of his body on her sheets for her to cry over in the night when the mozzies bit her and woke her up. He hadn't said see you later, or even see you, and she hadn't expected him to. She had known all along that he was going to leave. Not that it made it any easier to bear. And the unemployment benefit that was still arriving regular as clockwork in her bank account didn't seem to be that much any more after a couple of months of spending Michael's fifties.

By mid-morning she felt a little better, ate some yoghurt and a couple of slices of watermelon to take the sour taste out of her mouth. Then she went to the pub looking for someone to talk to. There was nobody on the veranda. Only Frank, sitting in his usual corner nursing a glass of beer and staring out over the salt scrub to where the grey clouds hung on the horizon. He jumped up when he saw her.

'What can I get you, young lady?'

'Hello, Frank.' she said. 'I just came in for a lemonade ...'

She got no further

When she came back she found a glass of lemonade, a small tot of some thick brown liquid and a basket of hot chips lined up in front of the empty chair at Frank's table. She sat down and sipped the cold lemonade. Nibbled carefully on one of the chips.

'Have some of this.' Frank held out the other drink. 'Just a sip, mind.'

She did as she was told. It went through her like an electric shock.

'What is it?'

'Just a bit of brandy.' And then, 'Does Michael know?'

She shook her head. Ate another chip. 'He's gone back to uni.'

'Are you going to tell him?'

She shook her head again. 'He's got his study to do. He won't want to be bothered with a baby.'

'What are you going to do then? Go home?'

'I can't go home, Frank. There's nothing there. No hot water. No electricity. How can I have a baby in a place like that?'

After six months in Black Rock, Collette could no longer imagine living without such things.

'I've got a bed.'

'Come off it, Frank. As if I'd want to move in with you.' And then, shaking her head. 'I'm not looking for a bloke. Not just at the moment.'

'No, no.' Frank laid his hands palms up on the table. 'That's not what I meant. Not what I meant at all.' He ran one hand through his thick brown hair. He reached out to take

Collette's hand but thought better of it. 'It's only a veranda. There's a cat on the bed. But you're quite welcome.'

And he smiled.

Frank had a long, lugubrious face upon which a lifetime of sun and drink had left their mark. Muddy eyes lost in deep lines. A large nose with narrow nostrils. A thin mouth covering strong teeth. But his smile changed everything. It was full of warmth and charm.

Collette found herself smiling back. The basket of chips was half empty. The brandy was gone. Her stomach lay unprotesting.

'Okay.'

Collette was sick twice on the way to Frank's place. The first time she made it to the toilets in the little park by the beach. Frank waited for her outside, leaning on his old black bicycle and watching the waves. The second time they were up on top of Black Rock. Frank took a folded handkerchief out of his pocket and wet it under a tap. He wiped Collette's face very gently and they stood for a while watching the great expanse of the ocean moving gently under the afternoon sky. But she ate a bowl of rice pudding at six o'clock, sitting at the table in Frank's kitchen while he sat at the other end reading the paper.

Frank's kitchen was the only room in the little cottage, apart from his bedroom and the veranda where Collette was to sleep. It was a large room with a table in the middle. There was a big wooden dresser against one wall, cluttered with books and tubes of paint. An old wood stove crouched by the back door. An old-fashioned arm-chair stood by the stove. A large black-and-white cat had possession of the chair

At eight o'clock, when Collette was thinking about going to bed, the man from the gift shop by the river came in carrying her clothes from the caravan wrapped in brown paper and tied up with string. He was dressed in a silk open-necked shirt and a pair of cream slacks, the canvas deck shoes on his feet the only concession to beach living.

'You should clear the path up to the road, Frank,' he said, reaching down and brushing sand off the hem of his trousers. 'It would make life easier for the rest of us. Mind you, it's a lovely night.' He shook Collette by the hand. 'The name's Curtis. But you can call me James.'

FIVE

On a warm September afternoon, Collette sat alone in the little garden in front of Frank's cottage. Out on the beach a cold wind was blowing the sand in pale drifts across the wet flats left by the dying tide. Off-shore a lone dolphin turned his back in the grey water. But in the garden the warmth lingered, sheltered by the tangle of banksia bushes and lantana that surrounded the area of rough bush grass that was the lawn.

Collette was sitting in the big armchair which had been dragged out from the kitchen, with the black and white cat crouched on what was left of her lap. In front of her was a table made from rough timber, covered with a white cloth. She was heavily pregnant.

Frank came out of the cottage carrying a laden tray and treading carefully over the rough ground. He began unloading the tray and setting the table with an assortment of old china.

'You can have the cup with the rosebuds on, seeing as you're the birthday girl.'

'You haven't made the tea yet, have you, Frank?' Collette struggled to sit up. 'Jim's not here. And you know how fussy he is about his tea.'

Frank shook his head. 'I don't know how you get away with calling him Jim. Nobody else can.'

There was the sound of a car on the road behind the house and a short time later James Curtis arrived. He had his market basket over one arm, a plastic supermarket bag in the other hand and over his head bobbed a large transparent balloon containing a pink teddy bear.

'Here we are then!' he said, putting the basket down on the grass and hiding the supermarket bag coyly under the table. 'No peeking until after tea. But you can have your balloon now.'

'I've never had a balloon before.' said Collette. 'How did they get the bear in? How will I get it out?'

'Wait for the balloon to go down and then you'll be able to have the bear. And it's for you, too. Not the baby.'

He bent down and began unpacking the basket. Plates of sandwiches and scones, a basket full of chicken wings done his special way, hot flaky rolls filled with spinach and cream cheese.

'Here's the tea.' he said, handing a paper packet to Frank, 'and don't forget to warm the pot first. I just have to go and get the cake.' And he hurried around the back of the house.

After tea, James got out the supermarket bag and gave Collette her presents, one by one. Silver ear-rings in a velvet box. 'I had these made especially. There isn't another pair like them in the world.' A fancy box, packed with talc and soap and perfume. 'It's nice and light.' said James. 'Just right for a young girl like you.' A china tea-pot, shaped like an English cottage. 'Now that's for your glory box.'

'What's a glory box?' said Collette, peering into the tea-pot, which was full of toffees.

'A glory box is where you put your bits and pieces. Table cloths and bed linen and such like. For when you get married.'

Collette giggled. 'I don't think people do that any more.'

The last parcel contained a tiny baby's dress made from fine cream wool, smocked across the yoke.

'I had that made, too,' said James, proudly. 'I was flat out finding someone who could do that smocking. It's a dying art.' He turned to Frank. 'Is everything okay?'

Frank nodded. 'Saw the doctor today. He reckons it'll be another week.'

'How did you get into town?'

'Walked.'

James sighed. 'Over that hill! I do wish you'd let me drive her. Any afternoon I'm free. You know that.'

'It doesn't do her any harm,' said Frank. He grinned at Collette. 'A bit of exercise does her good. Keeps the weight down.'

A week later summer arrived. Collette awoke to find the early sun had made a hot bowl of her veranda bedroom. The brightly coloured sarongs hung limp at the windows. Outside, the scream of the gulls mingled with the shouts of the surfers, running along the beach towards the base of the Black Rock where the waves rolled in perfect formation. Squeezed into her togs and wrapped in a sarong Collette went down to the beach and swam in the cool water

It was easy to forget about the baby, she thought, when you can lie in the water and look up into the blue sky and imagine yourself back to the way you were. All winter she had ignored it, living in Frank's cottage and walking on the beach, allowing the slow boredom to take her as the child grew and commanded her body. Now it was impossible to ignore. She was aware of the weight of it, the shining globe of her stomach where the baby lay tight packed beneath her skin, its movements as it probed her ribs and forced its head between her legs, hanging heavy as she walked. But now she lay weightless in the sea staring up into the blue depths of the sky while the gentle power of the waves lifted her body and rolled underneath.

Then she heard shouting – Frank's voice sounding thin and far away - and, looking up, saw the beach a long way off and Frank waving his arms at the water's edge.

She lifted her hand and waved back. 'It's okay.' she yelled. 'I'm coming in.'

She turned over and began to swim. But she had drifted out a long way and was exhausted and beginning to be frightened before she found herself lifted by a wave and carried to shore, to be dumped uncomfortably on the wet sand at Frank's feet. She rolled onto her back and lay breathless and laughing.

'You silly girl!' said Frank. 'What did you think you were playing at?'

She squinted up at him. 'I didn't realise how far out I was.'

He held out his hand. 'Come on, get up. You'll catch your death lying there. I'll make us a cup of tea.

But, after breakfast, she was up again, washing the louvres in the veranda, 'You should have seen the dirt when the sun came through them this morning.' And would have tackled the rest of the house, only Frank made her lie down and rest. In the late afternoon she came wandering into the kitchen where Frank was painting.

'Where are you off to now?'

'Just down the beach. I need some fresh air. It's stuffy in here. Go on, Frank. Let me!'

'Only as far as the rocks. And come straight back.'

He watched her cross the garden, stalked by the cat with his tail aloft, and then went back to his work. It was a new canvas and he had already sketched in the line of the horizon and the bulk of Black Rock. Another of his beach scenes that sold well enough in James' shop to be hung on walls up and down Australia by people who didn't know that they were shit. Or who knew it but enjoyed telling their friends that the painter was none other than Frank Duncan who used to be Inspector Darbyshire on TV, and how they had discovered him, a old drunk in a seaside town.

But, as he worked, this one was different. An afternoon sky, the tide out and the long shadows creeping across the sand. A glow from the dying sun, reflected in the wet sand. And a girl in a sarong, walking on the beach. A girl with untidy blond hair and a full belly.

Frank had never touched Collette. He'd brought her into his house like a stray pet and cared for her. But he'd never touched her. Apart from taking her hand to help her over rocks when they were walking on the beach or, now, to help her in and out of chairs. He had watched her sleeping when he came in from fishing late at night and saw her in the narrow veranda bed with the moonlight on her face and the cat hunched resentfully on her feet. Watched her in the armchair in the evenings when sleep took her unexpectedly and the book she was reading fell to the floor. Watched her in the garden hanging out wet clothes, standing on tip-toe to reach the line, her strong white arms lifted above her head.

Now as he drew the strong voluptuous lines of her body, as familiar to him as the shape of Black Rock, it was like he touched her. Like drawing his hands down the hard shape of her belly. Like touching his fingers to the soft hollows of her skin. Like holding her in his arms and feeling the warmth of her body against his. And, when he looked up, it was almost dark. And Collette was not there. He found her huddled on the rocks at the end of the beach, her eyes staring up at his.

'I think the baby's coming.'

It was cold now, the wind blowing strong from the sea, the sky covered with a thin layer of cloud which had snuffed out the last of the sun.

'What are we going to do?' Collette gasped and drew her knees up.

'We'll have to walk.'

He pulled her to her feet and drew her close. 'You're shivering.'

'I know. I feel awful.'

Together they began the long haul up from the beach and onto the road that went over the Rock and into town. For a while Collette walked strongly enough, pausing now and again when the pain took her to stand gasping and clutching her belly or lean her head against Frank's chest. Then she could walk no more and Frank took her on his back, her arms around his neck, and walked, bent double across the top of the Rock. It was raining now, a misty drizzle off the sea blowing like a silver sheet across the lights of the town lying below.

And then a gasp from Collette, bitten off, and a gush of warm liquid down his back.

'Oh, shit. What was that?' Collette struggled to be put down. "Sorry, Frank, I've wet my pants.'

'It's your waters breaking.'

'Waters breaking? What's that?'

'It means the baby's ready to be born,' said Frank. 'We'd better hurry.' And then, looking at her stricken face. 'It's okay. It's only a bit of wet. Don't worry about it.'

'I think I'll walk the rest of the way.'

'I'm going to get that bloody phone put on,' said Frank. 'James told me to weeks ago. Trust him to be right.'

Black Rock's hospital had been saved three years previously by overwhelming public protest and a spate of near-fatal holiday accidents. It lay on the road leading out of town, a huddle of brightly lit buildings, surrounded by a neat garden.

Collette was found an empty bed where she proceeded to deliver her son while Frank, dressed in a borrowed hospital gown, drank hot tea with a middle-aged nurse and a patient with a lacerated foot who didn't feel like sleeping.

Later he went to see her. She lay propped up on pillows, her hair in damp wisps around her face, while the baby, wrapped tightly in a blue-edged blanket, lay snuffling in a cot by the side of her bed. She was half asleep but opened her eyes when he came into the room.

'Thanks for looking after me, Frank. What are you going to do now?' She giggled. 'You look pretty silly in that gown.'

'I rang James. He's coming over to get me. We're going to the pub to celebrate.'

'He won't want to see me, will he? Tell him to come tomorrow. I might feel like seeing him tomorrow.'

Three days later Collette was ready to go home.

Frank stood with his back to the room, staring out of the window while Collette dressed her son in the smocked dress that James had given her.

'Look at the state of him,' she said, holding the baby up. He was a fine big round-headed baby with a fuzz of blond hair and he looked as though the dress was choking him. 'It must have cost a fortune and he's only going to wear it for half an hour.'

'Never mind,' said Frank, turning from the window. 'James'll be pleased. That's the main thing.'

'Yeah, Jim'll be pleased. He's all right, Jim.' Collette plonked the baby into the crib and sat herself down on the edge of the high bed. 'Who d'you think he looks like, Frank? Me or Michael?'

Frank walked over to the end of the crib and peered inside. 'Come off it, Collette. He's a baby. He looks like a little pink frog.'

'But he's got his dad's eyes, don't you think?'

'Don't ask me,' Frank pleaded. 'I can't tell. They all look the same to me.' He went back to the window. Leaned his shoulder against the wall. 'Are you going to tell him?'

'Michael? Why should I?'

'I'm sure he'd like to know he has a son. I would, if it was me.'

She shook her head. 'Forget it. He wouldn't be interested. Come on, Frank, let's go home. I can't wait to get out of this place.' And then, 'I can come home with you, can't I?'

Sudden panic at the thought of her going anywhere else. 'Where did you think I was going to take you?'

'I just thought I'd ask. It was never supposed to be for ever. And there's him now. You might not want to live with a baby.'

Frank smiled. Pushed himself away from the wall. 'I never thought I would at my time of life. But I expect I'll manage. Ready to go?'

Collette tipped herself off the high bed and reached into the crib for the baby. She held him out in front of her and stared at him. The baby, hanging hunchbacked in his mother's hands, yawned widely and blew a milky bubble.

'I'm going to call him Ian.'

'Why Ian?'

'I dunno. I just like it, that's all.'

Two months later Collette lay sleeping in a cane arm chair. The chair, a gift from James Curtis, sat in the corner of the garden under a poinciana tree which gave dappled shade. At her feet the baby lay on a rug, sprawled out like a skinned frog, his eye-lids fluttering. It seemed to be a permanent state for both of them, thought Frank who had brought his easel out into the garden to watch over them. Collette, when awake, had a habit of leaving Ian in the garden while she pottered about the house and Frank was constantly afraid that something might happen to him. Afraid the cat might sit on his face. Afraid of the magpies that walked on the lawn. Afraid of the people on the beach who might come into the garden and snatch him away.

He was painting her again, trying to catch the way the hot light fell on her face in golden pennies. The contrast between smooth white feet and the rough bush grass, turning brown under the summer sun. He hadn't painted a beach scene for months, not since the day Ian was born, and these new paintings were not for sale. He was living on the little bit of money he had in the bank and had never been happier.

After a while Ian stirred. His eyes opened suddenly and revealed a solemn stare. Then, deciding that he was probably hungry, he cried. Or rather, yelled a demand. That was more Ian's style. Collette woke. Bent down and hooked up her baby with practised ease. Unknotted the tie at the top of her sarong. The child turned his face to his mother's breast.

'Make us a cup of tea, will you, Frank?'

And Frank went, thinking of sharks.

When he came back, Collette had the baby slung over her shoulder where he lay sozzled, his eyes turned up in his head. She was still naked to the waist, her breasts milky white against the brown skin of her throat and arms.

Frank bent down and put the mug of tea on the ground by her chair. 'I want to paint you like that.'

Collette looked up at him. 'What d'you mean? You paint me all the time.'

'No, no. Like that.'

Collette looked down. 'You mean with nothing on? You've got to be joking!'

'There's nothing wrong with it. People do it all the time. I could go up to the TAFE college and do it, if I wanted to.'

'Off you go, then, if that's what you want to do. I'm not lying around in the nuddy while you paint me. You can forget that.'

'What if I paint you when you're feeding Ian? That'd be all right, wouldn't it?'

Sharks, he thought, sharks.

Collette shrugged. 'I suppose so. But not today. I've got to get the washing in.' She hitched up her sarong and tied it tightly around her chest. 'How are you going to sell pictures like that in Jim's shop? You'll have to put a pelican on my head. Or fish coming out of my tits.'

And so, while the GATT talks struggled towards their conclusion in Geneva, snow descended on the newly-liberated people of Moscow and debate on the Mabo legislation continued in Canberra, Collette lay in Frank's garden and allowed herself to be painted.

For Frank, it was an obsession, a sort of creative frenzy that he had felt only once before when he was a young man, barely twenty, and a rising star on the London theatre scene. A young man with his blood running thick and hot who was dazzled by the allure of the theatre world and his own talent which had put him there. Never did he expect to feel that frenzy again, nor wanted to. And yet here he was again with everything gone - eating, drinking, sleeping - and only the desire to paint left in their place.

And Collette? What was it about the girl that had aroused such passion? Was it the girl herself? Or was it because of what her body made him want to do. The paintings. Well, of course he desired her, too. With a fierceness he thought had gone for ever. But desire could be kept in check. Or so he told himself.

It was his first lesson in repertory theatre, learned in the late 'fifties when he was nineteen and on a tour of the English provinces with one of those so-called gritty reality plays that were so tame by today's standards it made him smile to remember them There had been a sex scene or at least a bed scene, with Frank and the female lead sitting together under a sheet in a double bed on dusty stages the length and breadth of Britain while they exchanged meaningful dialogue and tried not to laugh.

The female lead, a dark-haired girl called Christine, made it her business to sleep with all her leading men and she had an almost perfect record, her only failure being the one before Frank, who had been sleeping with the director, a great, grizzled man of fifty in dirty jeans and an old corduroy coat who sat at rehearsal three rows back, watching the stage with an eagle's eye.

Christine was twenty three with plenty to teach and she was amused by Frank's eagerness. She liked to whisper in his ear when they were on stage, to arouse him. Easy enough to do in those days but Frank learnt well the lesson of control. Between the sheets with Christine he kept an iron grip on rampant desire, despite her best efforts to distract him, for fear of the director's booming whisper coming from the gloomy depths of the theatre in front of them. 'Control yourself, dear boy. Let's keep our mind on the job, shall we?'

Somebody once told him, he forgot who, some old left-over actor with his voice gone from too much drink, and bronchitis every winter from living in cold boarding houses, sitting in a pub over a whisky or three to keep out the cold, that the trick was to think of something unpleasant, a sort of cold shower for the brain in place of the real thing. Frank had learned to imagine himself being attacked by sharks, a creature that a boy from the East End of London was unlikely ever to see, but which frightened him nevertheless. He had seen a shark's jaw once on a visit to the zoo - big enough to stand up inside and lined with rows of teeth - and it had become the subject of nightmares for years afterwards. Although it was a skill he had seldom been called upon to use during his years as Australia's favourite TV detective because, despite the fact that body parts of all descriptions were by then permissible fare on both stage and screen, Inspector Darbyshire had always been a family show.

SIX

On a Wednesday morning in early February Collette went shopping in Black Rock, leaving her sleeping son with Frank. Leaving her foot too, in a manner of speaking, because that was what Frank was working on. A painting of Collette's foot, small and white, resting on fine pale sand at the bottom of a shallow, sun-filled sea. He had got the fish right - nibbling at the wisps of flesh where the ankle had been torn away and swimming delicately through the half-moons of the nails. Now it was the light, the way the sun slanted through the water and made dancing dapples on the sand.

It was something that had absorbed him long enough to make Collette feel left out and, walking steadily along the beach towards town, she hoped that Ian would shout loud enough to penetrate the hard shell of Frank's self-made cocoon. She carried her bad mood over the Rock, ignoring the white glitter of the water and the shouts of the hang-gliders swooping lazily in the warm air.

Mr Jackson the bus driver, leaning against the brick wall of the ambulance station in the middle of the main street and smoking his third cigarette, looked up and saw Collette trudging along in the black shade of the shop awnings, her shopping basket on her arm. He sighed out the last of the smoke and pushed himself upright, grinding the rest of the cigarette beneath his heel. 'I've been looking for you.'

Collette looked up startled. 'Mr Jackson! What do you want?' And then, after a sudden thought. 'Is Mum all right?'

'Yeah, she's fine. She wants to see you, that's all. I've been watching out for you for a couple of weeks. Thought you must have moved on.'

Collette shook her head. 'I haven't gone far.'

'Bus is going in five minutes, if you want to come. I'll drop you at your gate.' He peered at her more closely. 'Doing all right are you?'

Collette, wearing a tee-shirt and a pair of shorts, leather sandals on her feet and her pale hair tied back with a twist of elastic, looked little different from the girl Mr Jackson had left in Black Rock just over a year ago. Apart from a fine gold chain around her neck, dancing silver ear-rings, and a certain air of quiet self-confidence that even she didn't know she had acquired.

She shook her head. 'I can't come now. I've got - people - who need to know where I am.' She hitched the shopping basket on her arm. 'Friday. Tell Mum I'll come on Friday.'

On the way home she picked up the newspaper and a pouch of tobacco for Frank, by way of saying sorry for her bad mood, and a cooked chicken for lunch. But Frank was not pleased. He knew how little money was left in the bank.

'It was my money,' said Collette, dumping her shopping on the table. 'I can spend it how I like.'

'Not when it's gone, you can't. What are you going to do then?'

'I've got my pension. Every fortnight.'

'That won't go far. Spending it like this.'

'Do some more of your shitty paintings then. Or sell some of these ...' She indicated the stack of canvasses leaning against the wall with their backs to the room.

'No ...' Frank moved, as if to protect them.

'Why not? I don't mind, if that's what you're thinking. Nobody's ever going to know it's me. I don't think there's a single one that's got all of me on it.'

'Just get the lunch, will you?'

Frank shoved the easel into the corner and sat down at the table with the paper. He wouldn't be painting again, not with Collette in this mood.

Collette went to the sink to fill the kettle. She peered over Frank's shoulder at the banner headline: SHAND'S TRIAL STARTS TODAY. One of the pleasures of buying Frank the newspaper was having him read out what he called the juicy bits. It made her feel like she knew what was going on in the world outside Black Rock.

'Is that him? What's he supposed to have done?'

She leaned closer to see the picture under the headline. A man in a dark suit standing on the steps of a city building. An unfortunate camera angle had a large palm tree apparently growing from the top of his head.

'No, that's his lawyer. Listen, "Mr John O'Shea, corporate lawyer, emerges from the Supreme Court after day one of businessman Adrian Shand's trial on corruption charges".'

But Collette wasn't listening. 'That's Michael's dad.'

Frank turned his head. 'What makes you say that?'

'His name's O'Shea. And he's a lawyer. What Michael said he was.' She pointed at the picture. 'And look at him, Frank.'

The photograph had given her a shock. To see Michael's face translated into that of his father. Michael's smooth rather childish face honed and hardened by age and experience. That strong peak of dark hair springing in exactly the same way from his father's forehead. And those eyes. Collette turned and saw them again in the face of her own child, sitting on her hip. She dumped him into the sink and began tearing lettuce. 'It's him all right.'

'You ought to ask him for money. This bloke.' Frank flicked the paper. 'He must have plenty. Ask him for some for Ian.'

'You've got to be kidding.' Collette was horrified. 'What does Ian need money for? He's all right as he is.'

'He might be all right now but what happens when he gets a bit bigger and needs a cot? What about when he starts school? Or gets to the age when he wants a bike.'

'I never had things like that.'

'Yes, but why shouldn't he? If there's someone who can afford to buy them for him.' Frank turned back to the paper. 'Listen to this. "The trial is expected to last for six weeks. Mr O'Shea, representing J & K Constructions of which company the defendant is a former director, is expected to receive in excess of one million dollars for his services." One million dollars, Collette! For six weeks' work.'

Collette was not impressed. 'So what am I supposed to do? Ring up this … this John O'Shea character and tell him his son gave me a baby? Why should he believe me? And, even if he did, why should he give me any money? A man like that.'

'Why shouldn't he? Ian's his grandson when all's said and done.'

'I'm still not doing it.' Collette threw the lettuce into a bowl and began dissecting the chicken. 'Anyway, he might come and take him away. Did you think about that?' She turned suddenly from the draining board, knife in hand.

'Take him away? Why would he do a thing like that?'

'When he sees how he lives. His own grandson.'

'With me, you mean?'

'No, no.' Collette never thought there was anything strange about her relationship with Frank. She waved the knife around the room. 'Just this place. I mean, it's not much, is it? For the grandson of that sort of bloke.'

'You can always move back to your mother's,' said Frank grumpily.

'That reminds me,' said Collette, coming to the table with the chicken on a plate. 'I saw Mr Jackson in town. He said Mum wants to see me.' She sat down with the damp baby on her knee, handing him a smooth bone to suck. 'Here, have some of this chicken.' She pushed the plate across the table towards Frank. 'Don't waste it.'

Frank grinned, aware he was being teased. He folded up the newspaper and laid it by the side of his plate. 'Pass the bread, will you, Collette? I'll make us a sandwich.'

'I'll go up on Friday. Catch the bus from town.' Collette got up and fetched the knife from the draining board.

'Well, if you won't phone this John O'Shea character, I'm going to write to him. What do you say about that?' And then, in answer to Collette's shrug. 'It's worth a try, Collette. You wouldn't say no to the money, now, would you? You can post the letter on Friday when you go into town.'

Collette's mother was in the cave. There was nobody in the kitchen so Collette walked around the side of the house looking for her. She saw the old ute half-packed with jars and bottles in big cane baskets and remembered it was market day. She started walking down the steep sloping paddock at the back of the house pausing halfway to enjoy the sight of the sunlit valley and the green curve of the opposite hill. Against the background of the cicadas humming from the trees, a whip bird called and was answered by his mate. Near the fence the goat stood in the thin shade of a half-dead wattle tree and gazed at Collette with remembered bile. Collette hitched the baby on her hip and walked the rest of the way down the hill and, finding the narrow path behind the shed, scrambled down the rocks until she arrived at the cave mouth, a dark yawn in the hillside with a narrow sandy shelf at the front.

Just inside the cave it was tall enough to stand up but further back in the cool earth-smelling depths the roof sloped steeply to meet the upward thrust of the floor. Along the sides were wooden racks which Nina was in the process of emptying of the jars of yoghurt and cloth- wrapped cheeses which were stored there. Now she straightened up and squinted her eyes to see Collette standing against the glare of sunshine.

'I'm glad you're here,' she said, by way of greeting. 'You can help me with this lot. It's market day today.'

Then she took a step forward. 'Who's this, then?' She stuck out a gentle finger for the baby to grab but he turned his face away and nuzzled into his mother's neck. He was not used to strangers

'His name's Ian.'

Nina peered at the baby. 'There's not much of you in him.'

'He looks like his father.'

Although his round firm body and neat limbs were enough like his mother but these were hidden in the folds of the sarong that Collette had slung around her body to support him

'Tell me about him later.' Nina turned back to the shelves. 'I've got to get a move on.'

When the ute was packed, the three of them got into the cabin and Nina drove into Ney Creek. She had never discovered how to adjust the seat to allow for her legs which were a good deal shorter than Cliff's had been, and she found it difficult to use the pedals and see out of the windscreen at the same time so her driving style consisted of breathtaking swoops and jerks as she did these two things in turn.

Ney Creek markets were held on the far side of town where the land sloped down to the river and there was a big green playing field behind the school. The field was surrounded by enormous shade trees under which the ground was bumpy with gnarled roots. However these were the preferred sites away from the glare of the sun and were jealously guarded by the regular stall holders.

By the time Nina and Collette arrived, most of the stalls had been set up and the field was full of colour and movement. Early shoppers were browsing up and down the aisles between the stalls, pausing at the junk tables to search through boxes of old books and records, or filling their baskets with fresh vegetables and hands of yellow bananas. It was already hot. The cool morning air had evaporated and the breeze was little more than a whisper, disturbing the bright triangles of colour on the kite-maker's stall and picking up swirls of dust from the path that went up the hill from the gate to the place where the food stalls were already tantalising the air with aromas of falafals and Mexican rolls.

Collette and Nina covered their trestle table with white paper and set out the produce in neat rows. Nina propped the old hand-painted sign against the front of the stall. 'Goats' milk products. Nina Flowers. Hill End Farm'. There were always people with allergic babies who liked to know where they could get fresh milk. To begin with it was too busy to talk. The crowd swelled, swirling up and down the narrow aisle and pushing against the stalls. Collette sat with her back to an old tree and fed Ian who was fretful and not inclined to settle. He was not used to noise and people, and swivelled his head around, his eyes like bright buttons.

A young woman from a neighbouring stall came over. She was tall and brown, dressed in a long skirt in some thin material and an embroidered waistcoat against which her full breasts strained. She had a felt pixie hat on her head and a quantity of chiming silver jewellery around neck and wrists and ankles. A brown baby, dressed in a silver necklace and a disposable nappy, sat on her hip. The woman squatted in the dirt next to Collette, fetched out her own big brown-nippled breast and offered it to her indifferent child.

'How old is he?' She nodded towards Ian who was lying on a rug kicking crossly.

'Five months. Nearly six.'

Ian was wearing a blue and white cotton sailor suit and a pair of soft leather shoes, bought by James Curtis on one of his buying trips to Sydney.

Leaving her breast hanging, the young woman held up her own child and stared at it intently. 'This one's the same I think.' She grinned at Collette and ambled off.

At lunchtime the crowds quietened down. Ian lay sleeping, sprawled out on the dusty rug. Nina gave Collette some money and told her to go up to the food stalls and get something to eat.

Collette went the long way round. She saw dolls and tools and carved camphor-wood boxes. Stained glass wind chimes turning in the breeze. Silver jewellery in glass cases. Home-made raffia hats and big-brimmed cloth ones decorated with silk flowers. A man selling brass door knockers and plaques saying Toilet.

When she came back she said to Nina, 'I saw a Red Indian.'

A lean-faced man in his late thirties. Sitting cross-legged on the ground. Two feathers stuck in the knot of his hair. Playing some sort of musical instrument and chanting in a high, colourless whine.

'That's Dave Wardell,' said Nina. 'He's a Brisbane boy. Went to Cavendish Road High, same as me.'

'You know him?'

'Recognised him as soon as I saw him.' Nina shrugged. 'If he wants to pretend he's a Red Indian, let him. What harm does it do? He's the closest most people around here will ever get to the real thing.' She took a bite of her kebab. 'And it's all authentic,' she said with her mouth full. 'I reckon Dave knows more about American Indians than anyone alive.'

Nina took another bite. Got up and served a customer. Sat down again.

'I saw some men a couple of weeks ago,' she said suddenly. 'Down in the paddock where Jenny used to keep those coloured sheep. Remember them? It's all lantana in that paddock now ... Two dollars fifty for the small ones,' she called out to someone standing at the stall. 'They had clip-boards and big plans rolled up and a thing like a camera on three legs.'

'Did you ask them what they were doing?'

'Oh, yes. They were quite friendly. Told me the land was going to be developed as a resort. Showed me the plans. Hotel. Cabin accommodation. A big open-sided dining-room, to catch the view. All very nice. Told me the council was selling the land for arrears of rates. The developer was going to pick it up at a rock-bottom price.'

Nina stopped talking. She waited for Collette to speak.

'Arrears of rates?'

'That's what they said.'

'Does that mean you should have paid rates? And you haven't?'

Nina nodded. 'I think so.'

'Why don't you just pay them?'

Nina sighed. 'It's too much money. Thousands. I went to see them in the council offices. They said they'd sent me notices.'

'What do you want me to do about it?'

'I thought you could lend me some money. That's all I want. A bit of money. Enough to get the council off my back and stop the sale going through. I'll pay you back.'

Collette shook her head. 'I haven't got any money.' She looked at her mother. 'Honest.'

Nina nodded towards the baby. 'What about the bloke you're with? His dad?'

Collette sighed. 'I'm not with a bloke. And Ian's dad doesn't know he exists.'

'Well you must be with someone.' Nina nodded at the baby again. 'Where did you get those fancy clothes?'

'I've got a friend. That's all. Just a friend.' Collette didn't bother explaining about James. 'And he's no use. He's a painter. Paints pictures he won't sell.'

In the late afternoon the market packed itself up and Nina and Collette drove home through thick golden shadows.

'I don't know why you're bothering about those rates,' said Collette. She was slumped in the passenger seat clutching her hot, dirty baby. 'If the council sells the land you can move into town. Get yourself a little house. With electricity.'

Nina stole a quick glance at her daughter out of the corner of her eye. 'But Collette, this is Hill End.' She slid back up the seat to take a look out of the windscreen. 'I can't leave it. What would Cliff say? You know how he felt about the place.'

Collette thought, it's not so much that she is living in the past. More that she is living in a present that no longer exists. She can't seem to see that Hill End is dead.

The sun was dipping behind the hills as the ute came up the road from the valley and Nina wrenched the wheel in a perilous turn that took them past the old milk stand and through the gate. Across the weed-strewn paddock still touched by golden sunlight, the old house squatted in black shadow.

Nina drove the ute around the house and parked it underneath in the thick, dust-smelling darkness that made the baby, half asleep on his mother's knee, yelp with fright. They climbed up the back stairs to where Fleur, the old cattle dog, stood on the top step squirming her delight at their return.

Nina had a pot of vegetable stew on the stove, cooking since the morning. She bent down to stir up the fire. She pulled the cork out of a bottle of peapod wine, one of the last of the vast numbers that John had left behind when he took himself and his sons to America to collect pumpkin varieties. She lit the lamp and the daylight faded. She sat down in the armchair by the stove, put her feet up on a stool and took the baby on her knee.

Collette sat at the table counting and rolling the market money and stowing it neatly in the old metal cash box she had retrieved from Nina's hiding place under her bed.

'He needs a bath,' she said, looking up.

'Hands and face'll do,' said Nina, caressing the baby with her small, work-hardened hands. Ian, tired and becoming hungry, sprawled on Nina's lap and watched his mother intently. He was enjoying his grandmother's attention and knew that he could get his mother to feed him any time he liked.

For a while, it was almost like it used to be. The smell of the stew on the stove. The sound of the lamp hissing, drowning out the tick, tick of the iron roof as it cooled down. Fantastic shadows on the walls as the two women moved around the kitchen. Knives and forks and plates on the long wooden table. But that was where it ended. When Collette lay down to sleep, sharing a saggy double bed with Ian, she missed the sound of the sea and the noise that Frank made, sleeping in the next room.

Collette and Nina did not return to the question of the rates until Monday morning when Collette stood on the front verandah in the hot early-morning sun, Ian on her hip and a basket of yoghurt and goats' cheese at her feet.

'I suppose I could ask Frank,' she said. 'About the rates, I mean. He's owned property. He might know more about it than I do.'

She was almost fond of Nina this morning and, knowing she was leaving, of Hill End too.

'Well, you'll have to hurry up about it,' said Nina. 'The auction's in less than a month. And let me know, huh? Keep in touch.'

SEVEN

On Sunday evening, James arrived at the cottage bringing with him the food that was left over from the week-end's trading. He had half a pavlova, a little dried around the edges, but laden with fresh fruit and cream and he was looking forward to seeing Collette's face when he gave it to her. The kitchen was in semi-darkness. Frank lay sprawled in the armchair by the fire, smoking a thin home-made cigarette and staring at the picture of Collette's foot propped up on the easel on the other side of the room.

'Where is she?' said James in alarm

'Gone home to her mother's.'

It sounded so comically melodramatic that James felt like laughing but one look at his friend's face changed his mind.

'When did she go?'

'Friday.'

'When's she coming back.

'Tomorrow. On the bus.'

'Well, then,' said James comfortably. He was loading food onto the table from his big market basket and stared doubtfully at the pavlova. 'I brought her half a pav but I suppose it'll be all right in the fridge until tomorrow.'

Frank sat up. The table was laden with food. A basket of sandwiches, cut in triangles, several large slices of quiche and a generous hunk of what looked like terrine, wrapped in bacon. The end of a leg of ham wrapped in a tea-towel. James bustled over to the sink and filled the kettle.

Frank realised suddenly he was hungry. 'How come there's so much food? There never used to be this much in the old days.'

54

He remembered Sunday evenings before Collette came. A few bent sausage rolls, a plate of dried sandwiches, the whisky bottle dominating the table.

'That's because I save it up,' said James. 'Hide it from the customers. I'm not having them gobbling everything up and nothing left for Collette. She enjoys her Sunday tea.' He poured the boiling water into the tea-pot and carried it to the table.

Frank ground the last of his cigarette into the ash tray by the chair, got up and put on the light. James, in the middle of slicing the ham, looked up and saw the painting. He dropped the knife and walked around the table.

'That's something.'

Frank moved quickly across the room, picked up the painting in one hand, twisted it around, and put it on the floor with its face to the wall.

'Never mind about that.'

'But it's good. Let me have another look.'

'No'

James shrugged. Sat at the table. 'Shall I be mother?' He poured the tea and pushed a mug across the table to Frank. Reached out his hand. 'Here, give me your plate. Do want some of this ham?'

The meal was eaten in silence.

Afterwards James got up and cleared everything away, covering the left-over food with cling-wrap and stowing it in the fridge, then piling the dirty dishes in the sink. He turned on the hot water tap, added detergent and watched the white froth bubbling up between the plates. Then he changed his mind, turned off the tap and crouched down, searching for the whisky bottle that lived under the sink.

Frank looked up. 'What are you going to do? Get me drunk and steal my paintings?'

'Something like that.' James poured whisky into two glasses, then pushed one across the table to Frank. 'What about letting me have a look at them? Only look, mind.'

Frank swallowed hungrily and felt the whisky travel down warm between his ribs. He waved his glass in the direction of the paintings. 'Go on then. If you must.'

James went across the room and put the paintings on the easel one by one, standing back to look carefully at each one. There was silence in the room, broken only by little grunts of approval from James and deep sighs from Frank slumped at the table with his nose in his glass.

Collette and the sea. The sea and Collette. And everywhere the glory of summer light on water and rounded limbs.

When he had finished, James walked back to the table, sat down heavily, and drained his whisky in a single gasp. 'You know they're very good, don't you?'

Frank shrugged.

'I mean, the ghastlies were never as bad as you thought. There's never been anything wrong with your technique. But these … I've never seen anything like them in my life.' He leaned forward. 'What does Collette think of them?'

Frank grinned. 'Not much. Nuddy pictures, she calls them.'

'And you?'

Frank sighed. 'I don't know, James. I'm just doing them, that's all.'

'But you have talent, Frank. More talent in your little finger than I've got in my whole body.'

'Talent? You want it? It doesn't do you any favours, believe me. Right now I'd sooner be painting than sitting here talking to my old mate. We used to talk for hours, you and me, didn't we? And now here I am on a Sunday night, full of dinner with the whisky bottle on the table and all I want is for you to go away so I can get on with it. I can't get the light right, that's the trouble. I've been at it all day.'

Frank looked over towards the easel where James, always meticulous, had replaced the unfinished painting.

'It's good, that.' he said with some satisfaction. 'I like that one.' He reached out and grabbed hold of the bottle, enveloping it in his big, hard hand. 'The whisky's good, too.' He poured himself another slug and waved the bottle in James' direction. 'It's a long time since I had a session with the whisky bottle. Collette doesn't drink. And I won't in front of her. It's bad enough as it is. She treats me like an old grey dog. Marginally better than she treats that baby of hers. So I'm not going to make myself into an old fool. More of an old fool than she already thinks I am.'

'She doesn't think you're a fool.'

'If she doesn't, she should. I am a fool. Look at me. Painting my heart out. Mooning over some kid young enough to be my daughter. Sitting in this damned shack and breaking my heart over things I should have left well alone.'

'You were happier before? Getting drunk and … and fishing?'

'Getting drunk and fishing. My oath I was.' Frank drained his glass and slammed it on the table.

'I'll make some more tea.' James filled the kettle carefully at the tap and lit the gas on the stove. 'Look, Frank, they're your paintings. You can do what you like with them. If you don't want the opportunity to make a name for yourself, don't bother.'

'Make a name for myself? I'm a household name as it is. Everyone's heard of Frank Duncan. Fat lot of good it's ever done me.' He emptied the last of the whisky into his glass then pushed the bottle away from him. 'Remember me? Frank Duncan? The first time you saw me? My name wasn't doing me much good that day, was it?'

It had been a spring day ten years previously when James Curtis dragged Frank Duncan off the pavement outside the old brick pub in the middle of town and took him home. He had been sleeping like a baby and obstructing the early morning shoppers out for their newspapers and loaves of bread. Not a pretty sight and a worse one for James who was one of Frank's greatest fans.

Frank, who had no recollection of anything that had happened to him during the three days since his arrival in Black Rock, remembered waking up to see a small, dapper man dressed in a dark suit and white shirt placing a cup of tea on the table by the bed. It was late afternoon by then and James, who was running a restaurant in Shelley Bay, was on his way to work

The mellow afternoon light, finding its way through thick lace curtains, showed dark, highly polished furniture set against cream painted walls upon which were displayed pretty water colours and fine embroidery framed behind glass. The bed was antique mahogany with mother-of-pearl inlays in the head and foot. The sheets were high quality white cotton and beautifully clean. The cover was heavy lace, to match the curtains, and was turned down to show a blue checked fine wool blanket under which Frank's body lay like a corpse. His hand confirmed what he already suspected. He was naked.

James, seeing the look in Frank's eye, said mildly, 'Your clothes are in the wash. There's a gown on the chair, if you want to get up. Please, make yourself at home,' and he left the room on silent feet.

The gown was red silk, embroidered with dragons, and several sizes too small but better than nothing at all while Frank prowled around a house furnished with the same ferocious good taste as the bedroom. He found the bathroom and lay for a long while in hot water before drying himself on a thick, white towel which seemed to have been left out for his convenience. There was nothing he could do about his wet footprints or the soapy ring around the bath which he thought were better left alone than wiped with the towel.

Later, prowling for food, he found the door. It was in the kitchen at the back of what had once been the alcove for the stove, hidden by a large green spider plant on a bamboo stand. A quick look out of the back door confirmed that an extension had been added to the house, an extension in which there were no windows. An air conditioning system was attached to the wall, dripping water onto the cracked concrete path.

The door was locked but Frank, who had picked up some odd tricks during his time as a TV detective, lost no time breaking in. It was a cinema. Thick carpet. Red velvet drapes. A grey screen taking up the end wall. The air as cold as ice.

Along one wall was a low wooden cabinet with narrow, slide-out drawers. Inside lay programmes for shows long gone. Autographed photographs of forgotten stars. All laid out under glass with their dog-eared corners straightened out. On the other wall, posters mounted back to back in hinged frames like a huge fan. In the middle of the room, a single chair like something you'd find in a dentist's room. A whisky bottle and a heavy glass tumbler on a table next to it. The projector took longer to find. Mounted in the ceiling, it was controlled by a panel set in the arm of the chair.

When James came home after midnight he found Frank sprawled in the chair, one leg hooked over the arm, his hand nursing a half-filled glass. The door to the kitchen was open, letting in the humid night air. All the lights were off. A stream of silver light from the projector threw an image onto the screen. For a moment he didn't know what to say. That his private world had been violated so wantonly made him almost speechless with rage. That it was one of his idols who had made himself at home in a place that was meant for nobody but himself gave him an acute pain just below his breastbone which he recognised as pleasure. In the end, saying nothing, he crept into the room and settled himself down on the carpet at Frank's feet.

'No, no. Don't move.' he said to Frank who was attempting to pull the silk gown across his lap.

The two men gazed at the screen. It was Richard III, made in the 1960s. A young Frank Duncan, dressed in badly fitting tights. His voice, full of power, seemed to fill the small, cold room. James had imported his speakers from the USA and fitted them in a particular sequence so that the sound was at its purest when it arrived at the chair in the middle of the room.

Frank, with his legs closed together like a maiden aunt, glanced down at his host and wished he was wearing underpants. Like most people, he assumed that James was gay and felt sure that, once the movie was finished, he would be called upon to sing for his supper in whatever form that might take, something he had not the slightest intention of doing. He didn't think he would hit him. Frank was not a violent man but thumping queers was something he didn't mind doing when the need arose. But on this particular occasion, dressed in no more than a skimpy dressing gown and with his clothes, wallet and car still in the possession of the queer, it seemed a less than sensible course of action.

Getting out was probably the better option but he had enjoyed sufficient of James' whisky to prefer the inside of his host's house to the outside.

But Frank was wasting his time. James was not interested in his body. Not the slightest. Or, at least, he was but only in the bits of it that might fall off or drip out during the course of his stay in the house. Hairs in the bath. Whiskers in the sink. Stains, from whatever cause, on the bed sheets. And he wasn't a queer either. Although he liked men well enough. He could talk to men. Be close to them, or close enough, without getting that feeling. The one he didn't like. The one he couldn't control. That was the trouble with women. Get close enough to talk to them and you could smell the perfume of their bodies, see the fine grain of their skin. And then there were the ones on the street. Their bodies on display for everyone to see. Breasts moving under thin clothes. Long thighs disappearing into skimpy shorts. A glimpse of soft flesh through a sweat-stained armhole, to look at whether you wanted to or not. Cigarettes and hamburgers devoured by warm mouths. Inhabiting the streets with their noise and chatter. And they didn't care. Laughed and brushed past him and didn't care.

So was it any wonder it was the screen women he loved? The truly beautiful, romantic women that lived on the wall in his air-conditioned room. Sophia Loren and Audrey Hepburn. Elizabeth Taylor with those glittering purple eyes. Ellen Browning who used to star with Frank, with her long, thick hair and a hint of challenge in her brown eyes. He didn't care for the stars that were making films nowadays. Skinny woman that showed everything. Ugly women with big eyes and wide mouths. Spreading their legs and tossing back their hair. A man grunting between their thighs. It wasn't what he wanted, that sort of thing. Not what he wanted at all.

When the film was finished, James climbed to his feet and powered down the room, turned up the air-conditioning a notch to clear the humidity caused by the open door, picked up the tray with the empty bottle of Scotch and the dirty glass, and motioned Frank to leave the room ahead of him.

'I've got some supper,' he said, locking the door firmly behind him. 'It's only leftovers, I'm afraid.'

The leftovers consisted of a rich, wine-flavoured stew followed by a couple of perfect crème brulée in a flower-patterned dish. Half a bottle of good claret, left behind by a customer, followed by fresh brewed coffee

'Do you know what happened to my car?' Frank stretched himself out in his chair and watched James fussing with the percolator. 'I can't remember where I left it.'

'It's with a panel beater. You wrapped it around a post.'

'Oh, yes, I remember. Someone gave me a lift into town.'

'What happened, Frank?' James carried the coffee pot carefully to the table. 'I can call you Frank, can't I?'

Frank waved his hand. 'Yes, yes. Call me what you like. Nothing happened. I just got drunk, that's all. Nothing unusual about that.'

'Yes, but why here. Why in Black Rock?'

'Is that what it's called?' Frank reached out his hand for his coffee, added a generous quantity of cream and brown sugar and stirred thoughtfully, slopping some of the hot liquid onto the table cloth. 'I was in Noosa. With my wife. I got tired of being there. That's all there is to it.' He looked up. 'You know Darbyshire's been cancelled, don't you?'

'I'd heard a rumour.'

'Well, it's true. They told me last week. Said I could retire. Spend more time with Patsy. Guest spots, now and again, if I wanted them. Great news, eh?' He lifted his top lip, showing strong brown teeth. 'The trouble is, I've got no money. And she's an expensive luxury, my word she is. Up and down Hastings Street. Drinking coffee with her chums. Propping up the bar with half of Melbourne, freshly fried from the beach.' He shook his head. 'Not a pretty sight, I can tell you.'

'So you left?'

'Went to the nearest second-hand dealer. Bought the car. What do you think of it, by the way? Not bad, eh?' The car was an orange Chrysler Valiant with white upholstery covered with tigerskin towelling. 'I didn't know where I was going to go. Looks like it was here.'

'Here?'

Frank grinned. 'Well, I'm retired. Why not here? It's the beach, isn't it?'

Over the next few days, galvanised by the thought of Frank settling down in his house and torturing him permanently with coffee stains and tooth paste spit, to say nothing of little splashes in front of the loo, James worked on the problem of finding somewhere for Frank to live. Finding the beach shack was a lucky break. Driving the orange monstrosity from the panel beater's he had stopped to get milk at the snack bar in town where he was accosted by a young man who wanted to know if the car was for sale. The young man, a surfie junkie drop-out sort of person, had a shack by the beach which he was willing to swap for the car which he wanted to drive to Western Australia, chasing waves. He had used the shack as crash pad for a couple of years and it was in a disgusting state. Frank was horrified when James showed it to him but he had little choice but to accept with as much cheer as he could muster.

It was James' personal triumph. Frank Duncan was in Black Rock, hiding in a hut by the beach, and nobody knew it but him. He read the papers with glee. Interviews with Patsy Duncan, the shattered look in her eyes due more to the state of the matrimonial bank balance, which Frank had stripped bare before he left Noosa, than the disappearance of her husband. Interviews with Frank's producer in Melbourne about his state of mind. Even a photo of the old Valiant, wrapped around a post on the highway. The ABC dragged out all Frank's old movies and played them in their Friday night spot, fronted by a sorrowful John Hines, his face more lugubrious than ever.

It was around this time that Frank decided to get on the grog and his appearance in the Railway Bar in Black Rock, looking relaxed and tanned, blew his cover and brought frantic phone calls from Patsy, holed up in the Melbourne house with a line of creditors at the door.

Well, it was all a long time ago. Frank the runaway celebrity had turned into Frank the local identity, better known for getting drunk and falling down than for his role in a forgotten TV series. James sometimes wondered if he ought to regret his involvement with the man.

But these paintings were something else.

He reached out and gave Frank a mug of tea into which Frank poured the remains of the whisky out of his glass.

'What about the paintings, Frank?'

'They're staying here.'

'But if people could only see them ...'

'They're not going to.' Frank's eyes were hard. 'Leave me alone, James. They're mine.'

'I understand,' said James. 'I know how you feel. Why you want to hide them away. If I'd done them I'd want to hide them away too. They're too ...' He was lost for words.

'Personal,' said Frank. 'They're too personal.'

'Yes, but don't you see? You owe it to people ...'

'Rot!'

James tried another tack. 'What about me? Don't you think you owe it to me?'

Frank looked up briefly. 'You? Why should I owe you anything?'

'Well, not me then. But what about yourself? Don't you owe it to yourself? I can't believe you'd pass up a chance to make a name for yourself as a serious artist. Not just the old drunk who used to be Inspector Darbyshire. Come on, Frank! This could be your last chance.'

Frank lifted his head. 'What if I don't want a last chance?'

James sighed. Had one last try. 'What about the money, Frank? I mean, if you're not painting the ghastlies and you're not selling these, what are you living on? Eh?'

'Take them!' Frank swept his hand across the table, knocking over his glass so it rolled in a semi-circle. 'You're quite right, of course. There isn't any money. And I need to get some canvasses. I haven't got any canvasses left to paint on.'

'I'll bring you some tomorrow.' James reached forward and removed the empty whisky bottle from the middle of the table. 'Go fishing, old love. Why don't you do that? It's a beautiful night. And Collette will be back in the morning.'

EIGHT

Frank sat in the kitchen with his feet up on the footrest of Ian's highchair, his long legs stretched across the doorway. Outside it was a hot midmorning but the kitchen was cool and gloomy, smelling of paint and milk puddings. Collette and Ian were on the beach, sitting in the water. The baby would come back, as he did every day, sleek, wet, brown and irresistibly beautiful. Frank was sketching on the back of an old envelope, pausing every now and then to suck the end of the pencil and think. He had decided to add a couple of rooms to the shack.

A few days ago he'd said to Collette, 'If we put a couple of rooms on the back, we can use my room as a lounge room. Have somewhere to sit at night, apart from the kitchen. And you and Ian can have a bedroom instead of sleeping on the veranda.'

'And a bathroom.' Collette said. 'A bathroom would be nice.'

Frank laughed. 'That's three rooms.'

But Collette was right. A bathroom would be nice. At the moment all they had was an old fibro shack at the end of the garden and a cold water shower by the back door.

Absorbed in his work, Frank didn't hear the sound of someone approaching until he looked up and there she was, blocking the breeze from the back door. A tall woman in late middle-age. Her hair a fashionable beige. Neat tailored shorts and a white shirt, open at the neck. Long, tanned legs which she was now examining carefully for scratches.

'Aren't you going to ask me in?'

Frank climbed reluctantly to his feet. 'If I must.'

The woman stepped into the kitchen. Looked around. Noted the highchair but said nothing. Only her eyebrow raised half a notch, a signal that Frank recognised instantly.

'Got a drink?'

'I'll put the kettle on.'

She pulled out one of the chairs and sat down, resting her elbows carefully on the table, as if expecting to find something sticky. 'Well, you're quite the artist, now, aren't you Frank? I've been seeing your stuff all over town. Monique has one in her living room She's redecorated the whole room, just to match the painting. It looks very smart, I must say.'

'What do you want, Patsy?'

'I just thought I'd come and see you. A wife's entitled to see her husband, isn't she?'

'From Melbourne? You've come to see me from Melbourne?'

Patsy shrugged. 'I'm on my way to Noosa. So this is on my way. But, God, it's the back end of nowhere, this place, isn't it? I don't know how you can stand it. Not a bad bit of real estate, all the same. Beach front's worth a fortune, these days. Even in a place like this.'

'You keep your hands off. This is mine.'

'Yours and who else's, that's what I'd like to know. And don't tell me you've got a child, Frank. What am I supposed to say? Congratulations?'

Frank took two steps across the room. Patsy sat still, a glint of triumph on her face, and watched Frank's hand stop in mid-flight and, for want of something else to do, thump down, open-palmed on the table between them.

'It's none of your bloody business what I do.' He thrust his head forward. 'I settled up with you years ago. You've got everything you're going to get out of me.'

'That's a fine way to speak to a wife you haven't seen for ten years.' Patsy stared down at her hands and made some fine adjustments to the numerous gold rings she was wearing. 'We are still married, you know, Frank.'

Frank grunted. 'Married because you like the name Duncan too well to give it up. And because I can't be bothered thinking about you long enough to do something about it. And now, just because I've sold a couple of paintings, Patsy wants to play happy families. Is that what this is all about? Fancy yourself at the exhibitions, do you? Champagne and orange juice and little red stickers? Because you can forget it. Hear me? Forget it!'

'I thought you might give me a painting.' Patsy's attention strayed from her rings to the polish on perfectly manicured nails. 'I still have people in, you know. When I can afford it. It'd look a bit funny, don't you think, if I didn't have one of my husband's paintings on the wall? Sort of pinky colours, if you can manage it. To tone in with the room. I can't afford to redecorate.'

At that moment Collette walked in with the baby half-asleep on her hip. She paused in the doorway while her eyes adjusted to the gloom and saw several things at once. A smart woman sitting at the table as if she owned the place. Frank standing, fists clenched, his face tight with fury. The kettle boiling its head off in the corner of the room.

Frank looked up. 'Make some tea, will you, Collette? We'll be in the garden.'

He took two steps around the table, grabbed the woman by the top of her arm, yanked her to her feet and marched outside.

Patsy, pleased that she had not lost the knack of driving Frank into a fury, settled herself into Collette's cane armchair, stretched out her legs, admiring her new gold sandals that managed to hide the fact that her feet were too big and bony to be attractive, and prepared to press home her advantage.

'Well, that explains the fat sheila in the pictures,' she said, nodding towards the house. 'A bit young, though, isn't she? You could be her father. Her grandfather, come to that.'

Frank stood with his back to the garden, staring at the sea glittering under the hot sky.

'She's just a friend,' he said, from between gritted teeth. 'That's all she is. Just a friend.'

'And I suppose you're going to tell me that baby came from the fairies? Pull the other one, Frank.'

Collette came out of the house, stepping carefully on small bare feet, carrying a full tray which she dumped on the old table. She unloaded cups and plates, tea and milk. She went back into the house and brought a plate of buttered scones and another one of blueberry muffins, Jim's latest thing. The baby hung in her arms, grinning. He had been on his way to bed and was delighted to have a reprieve. Being used as a pawn in some game the adults were playing was better than sleep any day.

'Come and have your tea.' she said to Frank. 'You hold Ian while I pour.' She dumped the baby in his lap, then turned to Patsy. 'Milk or lemon?'

Despite his anger, Frank suppressed a grin. Collette was strictly a milk and two sugars girl. Where on earth had she learned about lemon?

It was this pretty scene that met John O'Shea's eyes when he floundered through the soft sand at the top of the beach and entered the garden. He had come the long way around, leaving his car on the Rock, and walking along the beach. He thought he had dressed for a day at the coast and was certainly a good deal less formal than he was every other day. Even so, linen slacks and an Italian knit shirt, silk socks and cream canvas shoes were a bit much for Black Rock. And he could have done with a hat. He stepped gratefully into the shady garden, his hot feet sinking into cool grass.

'I'm John O'Shea.' he said, his eyes searching the little group sitting around the table. 'I'm looking for Collette Flowers.'

This time Patsy's eyebrow went up more than a notch. This was good. Oh, yes, this was definitely worth wading through the bush to see. One look at Frank's face told her that something very interesting was about to happen. She settled back to see what it was.

Frank stood up, tucked the baby under one arm, and held out his hand. 'I'm Frank Duncan,' he said, and the two men shook hands. 'This is Collette ...' He indicated a small, blond, bare-footed girl, her ample body swathed in a twist of colourful cloth, standing behind the table and clutching the teapot as if her life depended on it. 'And this is Ian.'

The baby lifted up his head and grinned at his grandfather. He had been given a bit of scone to chew on and his face was smeared with butter.

'I'm Patsy Duncan, Frank's wife.' Patsy reached up and offered her hand. 'It doesn't look like he's going to bother introducing me.'

'Sit down and have some tea,' said Frank. 'Go and get another cup, will you please, Collette?'

And Collette escaped, scuttling across the garden and into the house to hide her burning face.

John turned politely to Pasty. 'Are you on holiday, Mrs Duncan? I was under the impression you were based in Melbourne.'

'I'm on my way to Noosa. I just called in to pick up one of Frank's paintings. He's enjoying a bit of a revival at the moment. His own exhibition next month. Isn't that right, Frank?'

You don't get to be a Queen's Counsel without learning how to read people with a fair degree of accuracy and John, well aware of undercurrents here with which he had no wish to involve himself, said merely, 'Noosa's a pleasant spot. I have a unit there myself.'

Collette came out with an extra cup, dumped it on the table, took her smeary son from Frank, and went back into the house.

'I think perhaps, after tea, you might enjoy a walk,' said Frank to John. He had no intention of this business becoming lunch-table gossip in Melbourne. 'You've already seen the beach. Ask Collette to take you up the bush track. The view from the top is worth the effort.'

Taking his cue from Frank, John settled down to drink his tea. And Patsy found out that, if you want to extract information from someone, a barrister is not the best person to choose. He spoke pleasantly to Frank about the cricket and answered Patsy's questions politely but revealed absolutely nothing about himself or the reason for his visit.

When he had finished his tea he said to Frank, 'I think might take you up on the offer of that walk,' and Frank got up and went into the house to find Collette.

She was in the kitchen, washing up with fiendish energy.

'Collette, I want you to take Mr O'Shea up the hill. Talk to him. See what he has to say.'

'I can't. Ian's not asleep.'

Frank went into the veranda, lifted the wide-eyed baby out of his cot and slung him over his shoulder.

'I'll look after him,' he said, going back into the kitchen. And then, before Collette had a chance to speak, 'And, no, he doesn't need feeding. He's fit to burst as he is. Now, go on. Let me have him. At least if I'm holding Ian I won't be able to hit her.'

Collette shrugged, hung up the tea towel and went out of the back door to where John O'Shea was waiting for her at the beginning of the path.

'I had your letter,' John began as they toiled up the steep slope towards the road. 'I must say it surprised me.' He watched Collette's back as she climbed the hill ahead of him. 'Are you sure the child is Michael's?'

Collette stopped. Turned around. 'Of course he is. I was with him all last summer.'

Which wasn't really the answer John was looking for but he found himself reluctant to press the point. Because, although he had been anticipating a situation of this nature at some stage in his son's career, Collette was certainly not the sort of girl he'd expected Michael to get himself mixed up with.

He had encountered Michael's girls from time to time in his flat. They were self-possessed young women with straight looks and little to say – to him, at least - and far too smart to end up in Collette's position.

But then, after Collette's letter arrived, he had spoken to his son and had been surprised by the fleeting look of joy on the boy's face, quickly suppressed, and the admission, freely given, that he could indeed be the father of Collette's child.

'But you didn't tell him? Why was that?'

'I didn't think he'd be interested.'

They arrived at the top of the path and Collette led the way up the narrow road, her small, bare feet stepping nimbly on the grass verge. After a while the bitumen was replaced by a sandy track sheltered by stands of banksia and tall old gums, gnarled by the wind. In between grew cycads and tree-ferns, worth a small fortune in city nurseries.

'But you wrote to me. Why did you suppose I'd be any more interested than my son?'

Collette stared at the man's bland face. 'It was Frank's idea. We saw your picture in the paper.'

Which explained the handwriting, John thought, which had been a beautiful copperplate, done with a thick-nibbed fountain pen. And the quaint old-fashioned language which was certainly not the sort of thing they taught in schools these days.

'And it's money you're after, is it?' Knowing perfectly well that it was but enjoying the look of intense misery on the girl's face. Let her work for it!

'Frank said ...'

'Frank said? What did Frank say? That I was rolling in it? Why don't you ask him for money? He must have some. I've seen what those paintings of his fetch.'

'Frank's just a friend,' said Collette stiffly. 'We share a house. We're not together or anything.'

'You pose for him.'

Collette felt herself blush. 'Yes, but he pays me. It's a business arrangement.'

'Pays you?'

'Frank says it's a perfectly respectable profession. When he started selling the paintings he rang up the TAFE college in town and found out what the pay is. Twelve dollars an hour, I make. So there's nothing iffy about it, if that's what you're thinking.'

Leaving John to follow her, Collette turned and walked up the steep path. By the time he caught up, trying hard not to pant, she was squatting at the end of a long wooden ramp jutting out from the hill, which was used as a launching platform by the hang glider pilots. No hang-gliders were flying, it being the middle of the week, and the air currents along the face of the cliff were in the sole possession of an eagle that twitched its wings to come closer and stare at them with a wild, yellow eye.

John walked carefully down the hot wooden boards and stood behind her, legs slightly apart, and squinted at the view through half-closed eyes.

'Where's Frank's place? Relative to where we are now?'

'Below us to the left. Look, you can see his roof.'

John followed the line of Collette's pointing finger and located the rusty iron roof gleaming dully in the carpet of green trees. 'Well, he's certainly got himself a good spot. Beach front properties are hard to find these days.'

'Now you sound like her,' said Collette scornfully. 'That wife of his. Stupid cow.'

There followed a moment's silence while John waited for a certain breeze to come back and cool his face which was still very hot from the climb and Collette mulled over a thought that she had suddenly discovered buzzing around inside her head and wondered whether she had the nerve to voice it.

Finally she said, 'Do you know anything about real estate, Mr. O'Shea?'

John nodded. 'A little bit. What do you want to know?'

'It's to do with rates. There's money owing on the place where my mum lives and the Council's going to sell it, if she doesn't pay. I just thought you might know what she should do.'

'So it's free advice you're after now, is it?' John crouched next to the young girl. 'What is it, a house?'

Collette shook her head. 'No, it's quite a big property. Up in the hills. I told her she should let them sell it. Get herself a little house in town. But I think I was wrong. It's like Frank's shack. His wife comes along and all she sees is beachfront real estate. Somewhere to put a block of flats and make a profit. But it's Frank's place.' She shrugged. 'I can't really explain it. And Hill End's the same. I can't imagine Mum living anywhere else.'

'So what do you want me to do about it?'

'Fix it up so she doesn't lose the farm.' Collette turned her head and gazed at him. 'I won't ask you for anything else, I promise.'

John smiled at the girl, switching on the charm which was a well-used courtroom strategy. 'So you don't want my money after all?'

Collette ignored the charm, an O'Shea trade-mark with which she was completely familiar.

'No, we'll manage. Don't you worry about us.'

'Well, then, I'll see what I can do.'

John stood up and reached down his hand to help Collette to her feet. He had already made up his mind that he would help her. It would be a small enough job and would certainly save him a lot of bother, to say nothing of expense, if this was indeed all the girl wanted from him. And it would satisfy his curiosity, which was well and truly aroused. A property in the hills, eh? He knew what they were beginning to fetch, even this far south, as development spread out from the Gold Coast strip.

'What happens now?' said Collette when they came to the narrow path leading to Frank's house.

'I'll let you know. Have you got a number where I can reach you?' And then, in response to Collette's puzzled look. 'A phone number. I'll ring you up.'

Collette thought for a moment and then said, 'Ring James Curtis. He's Frank's agent. He can give me a message.'

Frank and Patsy were still sitting in the garden amidst the debris of the tea things. Ian was asleep on Frank's chest.

'I'll be in touch.' said John, shaking Collette by the hand. 'Would you like a lift somewhere?' he said to Patsy. 'My car's parked just along the road.'

Patsy got to her feet and, ignoring Frank, walked away from the table. 'Just take me to the nearest pub. I'm dying for a drink. I'm up to here with tea. Tea!'

'Maybe there's none in the house,' suggested John, taking her elbow and steering her rapidly around the side of the house.

'If he doesn't have a bottle of whisky under the sink, it'd be the first time ever. Don't be fooled by the way he lives, Mr O'Shea. He's always got a bit tucked away, has Frank. It's getting it out of him that's the problem.' She started climbing the hill, her voice floating load and clear through the trees to where Frank stood in the kitchen doorway with his hands clenched hard at his side. 'Those paintings of his are fetching two grand in Melbourne for a start and don't tell me that's all taken up in commission ...'

Collette, coming into the kitchen with a tray loaded with the tea things from the garden, dropped the tray on the table and walked over to the doorway. She took Frank's hand. Gave it a little tug so that he looked down at her.

'Come on, Frank. Come to bed.'

NINE

In the late afternoon of the following day John O'Shea drove out of Ney Creek and took the narrow road that lead into the hills, following the line of the looping tree-lined creek until he crossed it by the old wooden bridge and left it behind. The road was the same one travelled by Mr Jackson, the bus driver, and would lead John eventually to the old wooden milk stand at the entrance to Hill End.

John had spent the previous night in Black Rock, staying in the motel and eating pizza at the only half-decent restaurant in the place before strolling up onto the Rock itself where he spent a long while watching the movement of the moon-lit water and thinking. It was of Michael that he thought. Although there were a couple of boys amongst the brood of children produced by his young wife, Naomi, it was always of Michael that he thought. His first-born child. Born of hope and expectation as first-born children always are and doomed to disappoint as they usually do.

The following morning he drove to Ney Creek. At nine-thirty he entered the offices of the Shire Council in the main street and approached the counter behind which stood a smartly dressed young girl with a worried expression on her face. According to a badge pinned to the pocket of her blouse, her name was Sharon. Her expression did not change when he requested a rates search of the property known as Hill End.

'It'll cost you sixty dollars,' she said anxiously. 'What do you want to know?'

'Everything,' said John, reaching into the inner pocket of his jacket,

Quite quickly Sharon returned to the counter and handed John a computer print out. John took his reading glasses out of his top pocket, perched them on the end of his nose, and proceeded to read over the top of them with the paper held at arm's length.

The land was registered in the name of Clifford Mander. There was quite a bit of it, some forty acres backing onto State Forest. It was zoned rural. There was no town water, nor power, and no easements marked on the sketch map except for one in the bottom corner, near the creek, which John assumed was for drainage. Three years' rates were owing to the Council, an amount of a little under two thousand dollars.

'How about a name search?' said John to Sharon who had remained on the other side of the counter, watching him read.

'A name search?'

'Find out if Clifford Mander owns anything else. You can do that, can't you? I suppose it'll cost me another sixty bucks.' He grinned and made a move for his wallet.

'I'll tell you, if you like,' said Sharon, moving closer and dipping her head towards his. 'No need to pay out again. I know what Mr Mander's got. Everybody does.' She nodded out of the big windows. 'See the shops over the road? He owns them. There's a couple of acres by the river, too. You know he's passed away, don't you? He was a nice bloke, Mr Mander. I liked him.'

'What about these other places?' asked John. 'Are the rates owing on them too?'

Sharon nodded. 'They're not up for sale yet. It's just Hill End. They've got a buyer, see? It's going to auction and if nobody else is bidding they'll get it for next to nothing. It's a pity, I reckon. I mean, Hill End's always been the same. We go there for picnics sometimes, me and my boyfriend.'

'Is there someone I can see about it?' John opened his wallet, extracted a business card, and handed it to the girl. 'I act for Mrs Nina Flowers. She's the executrix of Mr Mander's will.'

Sharon looked up at John and smiled. 'You're going to sort it out then? That's good oh. I'll go and fetch Mr Cross.'

Mr Cross, an untidy middle-aged man with grey skin and a balding head, was not pleased to see John O'Shea. With the business card held between finger and thumb, he escorted John into a small office with grey vertical blinds screening it off from Sharon's curious gaze.

John sat opposite him at the big desk, drew his cheque book from his inner pocket, took out his pen and clicked it open.

'I'm here to pay the rates on Hill End,' he said, the pen poised. 'I trust you will take my personal cheque? I am not yet at liberty to withdraw funds from Mr Mander's estate.'

He unfolded the search and laid it out on the table.

'Just the amount shown here? No extra charges? Late fees? Anything of that nature?'

Mr Cross shook his head.

John wrote the cheque. Tore it from the book. Waved it gently in the air, an action left over from his fountain pen days, and handed it across the desk.

'I'll get you a receipt.' Mr Cross stood up and went to the door. 'Sharon!'

'Are you in habit of selling off land without advising the occupier of your intention?' said John, when Mr Cross was back in his seat.

'Occupier?' said Mr Cross. 'There is no occupier. There's only that old goat woman and she should have been off the place years ago.'

'That old goat woman is my client,' said John, gently. 'She's the beneficiary of Mr Mander's estate. In other words, she owns the place and is not pleased at having it sold from under her. You did send out the notices required by law, did you not, Mr Cross?'

Mr Cross' skin went a shade paler. 'Notices were sent out.'

'But not to Hill End?'

'Not to Hill End, no. To Mr Mander's business address.'

'Which I presume is the bank over the road.'

'The bank. As you say.'

'And it never occurred to you to let Mrs Flowers know?'

'There's nothing in the by-laws to say I should.'

'Well then, it's just as well I came along.' said John, pocketing his pen and folding the receipt into his cheque book. He got up. 'No, no. Don't disturb yourself. I'll see myself out.'

Sharon lifted the flap in the counter to let him out.

'Mr Cross is not a happy man.' said John, with a nod of his head. 'I think you ought to make him a nice cup of tea.'

'I'm not surprised he's not happy,' said Sharon. 'I reckon he was going to make a few dollars out of that sale himself.'

'You're probably right,' said John. 'Make that tea, Sharon. Pour it down his front, that's what I'd do.'

Sharon grinned. 'I think I will. See you, Mr O'Shea.'

John walked across the wide, baking street and went into the bank. He wondered if he would find another version of Sharon who would answer his questions just because he asked them and not wonder why. The girl behind the counter was small and dark, a tiny engagement ring gleaming on a plump finger

He handed her his card. 'I've come to pick up Mr Mander's papers.'

The girl opened her eyes wide. 'I hope you've got a car,' she said, peering around him into the street beyond the big windows. 'There are plenty of them. Hold on a tick.'

She left the counter and disappeared into a back room, emerging some time later with several cardboard document boxes held in her arms. She dumped them on the counter. They were full to bursting with scruffy, dog-eared lids. Each one was marked with a number and a date written in thick marker pen.

'Hang on and I'll get the rest,' said the girl walking quickly to the back of the office.

When she came back, burdened by several more of the boxes, a young man with thinning hair came to the door of one of the screened-off offices.

'What's going on, Kate?'

'Oh, Mr Slater, there's a gentleman here who's come for Mr Mander's papers.' The girl was a little breathless. She dumped the boxes on the counter and handed the young man John's card which she had been holding in her teeth.

Mr Slater raised his eyebrows.

'I'm acting for Mrs Nina Flowers,' said John smoothly. 'She's the executrix of Mr Mander's will.'

'You've seen a copy of the will?'

John shook his head. 'The will is in one of these boxes.'

'Not your normal field, this, Mr O'Shea?' said Mr Slater, glancing at the card in his hand. 'It says here you're a corporate lawyer.'

'I'm a friend of the family.'

'Strange that you should turn up now. Mr Mander's been dead for some time.'

John inclined his head. 'Naturally I assumed that matters had been attended to. That Mrs Flowers had received advice from those best able to give it to her. Apparently that is not the case.' His blue eyes stared into those of the young man behind the counter. 'And, from what have been able to ascertain so far, it's just as well I have turned up. The matter of the rates on Hill End in particular required urgent attention.'

'Ah, yes. The rates.' The young man stared over John's shoulder at the Council offices across the street.

'A bad business.' said John. 'Very bad. It's a disgrace things have been allowed to reach such a point.' And then, with a change of tone. 'Now, what about these papers? Can I take them?' He reached out and put his hand on the lid of one of the boxes.

Mr Slater was silent for a moment. 'You can look at them certainly,' he said finally. 'I'd be glad if you did. But I don't feel I ought to release them to you for the time being. Not until you've had a chance to look at the will.'

'Quite right too,' said John, which broke the serious expression on the young man's face.

'There's an office you can use, if you like. It's down the back.'

Together they carried the boxes through the bank, past the sink by the back door where the tea was made and into a small dark room next to the toilets.

Mr Slater turned on the light.

'It's not much, I'm afraid. We've been using it as a storeroom.'

There was a bank of grey filing cabinets against the back wall with a couple of desks pushed up against them upon which rested a dismantled computer and a couple of old electronic typewriters. Shoved under the desks were several plastic bags full of Christmas decorations. Chairs were stacked in a corner with a dusty dried flower arrangement resting on the top one. There was a phone on the carpet, attached to the wall by a long grey cord.

John reached forward and twitched the wand on the blinds to reveal industrial bins and parked cars, a far cry from the view of river and hills from the window of his twentieth storey office in Brisbane. The sun slanted into the room, stirring the cold air.

Kate cleared one of the desks and John helped her heave it into the middle of the room. He pulled up a chair and sat down.

Kate grinned at him. 'I'll make you a cup of tea.'

It was after two o'clock when John walked out of the bank onto the hot afternoon streets, frozen to the bone and more hungry than he had ever been in his life. He drove out of town and found a little park by the river, stopping at a snack bar on the way to buy himself a sausage roll and a pile of chips. The park was empty of people and he took possession of a picnic table as close to the river as he could get where he laid out his food on its white-paper wrapping.

He smiled at the thought of his wife's face, if she could see him. She would have packed him something altogether more suitable - a pita bread stuffed with salad, one of the kids' all-juice poppers and perhaps a piece of her special wholemeal zucchini slice guaranteed to clean the system from top to bottom like lava flowing down a mountainside. Sometimes John wondered how his children survived so ferociously healthy a diet. When he had finished eating and had thrown the crumbs to a kookaburra which had spent the entire meal watching him closely from a nearby tree, he went back to the car, turned on the air-conditioning and closed his eyes.

One of the reasons John was so successful as a barrister was because he was prepared to follow his instincts. But never had his instincts led him as far as they had that day. What he had discovered was nothing short of extraordinary. Collette's mother, the so-called old goat woman of Hill End, the helpless widow about to be kicked off her land for arrears of rates, was worth in excess of one million dollars. And that was a conservative estimate. Clever manipulation of her share portfolio and judicious development of her assets could double an estate which had been lying stagnant for three years. And then there was Collette, penniless Collette, living in a beach shack with Frank Duncan the drunken once-upon-a-time TV star. Penniless Collette reduced to writing begging letters for the price of a cot. That young woman would be worth a fortune one day. And the child. Michael's child. His grandchild. Well, he'd done the child a bit of good after all and it wasn't going to cost him a cent. In fact, he'd done them all a bit of good, one way and another. And now he must summon up the energy to drive up the mountain and tell the old goat woman about her good fortune.

John sat up and turned the key in the ignition.

The house was almost in shadow, about to drown in the great black shape of the mountain. The heat of the day claimed John as he climbed out of the air conditioned car which he'd parked at the bottom of the front steps. It was dusty, too, and he began to wish he'd gone straight back to Black Rock and left this chore until the morning. He would be showered by now and enjoying a drink. Something with ice. Something alcoholic with ice. Definitely something alcoholic.

There was nobody home. Or, at least, nobody to answer his knock on a door that looked as if it hadn't been opened for years. After a while he walked around the side of the house where the land sloped steeply away, past a fenced-off vegetable garden where stands of banana and paw-paw stood guard over rows of tomato plants drooping on stakes and a lively patch of pumpkin vines growing in a tangle. Several chickens were loose in the garden, scratching in bare dirt. Further down the slope, with the lowering afternoon sun hot on his face, he came to a shed crouched in the corner of the field under the black shade of a mango tree. A small brindled dog, curled up in a hollow among the tree roots, looked up at his approach and thumped its tail.

Below his feet was the sound of singing but before he could investigate further, a woman appeared on the steep path on the far side of the dry-stone wall that marked the boundary of the field. She was small, with smooth dark hair pulled up on top of her head. She was wearing a white cheesecloth blouse with embroidery on it and a flowing loose-woven skirt, dyed in bright colours and tucked up somehow so that it was out of the way of her bare feet. She had a cord around her waist, decorated with silver and little bells. She was carrying an empty basket in one hand and a couple of old metal buckets in the other. She looked nothing at all like the old goat woman of John's imagination.

'Mrs Flowers?'

The woman looked up swiftly. 'You startled me.'

'Here, let me help.' John reached out his hand and took the milky-smelling buckets then offered the woman his other hand to help her over the wall.

'You are Mrs Flowers?'

The woman's hands went to her hair, smoothing the stray bits away from her face. Her skin was smooth and tanned, her body compact, like a young girl's. It was hard to imagine she was Collette's mother.

'I'm Nina Flowers.' She reached out her hand for the buckets. 'What can I do for you?'

'I've come about the land …'

'The land?' The buckets fell with a clatter. 'Hill End? It's gone then? How long have I got?'

'No, no. It's fixed up. I fixed it this afternoon.'

'Fixed up? What d'you mean fixed up?'

'I paid the rates.'

'You paid them? What's going on? Who are you?'

'I'm sorry, I should have said. I'm John O'Shea. Your daughter Collette sent me. You see, I'm her baby's grandfather.'

'Ian's grandfather? You are?' Nina tipped her head back and laughed. 'Well, that means we're related, in a sort of a way. You'd better come up to the house.'

She picked up the buckets from where they had rolled and began the long walk up the paddock with John by her side, matching his pace to hers. At the top he turned around and stood watching as the last rays of the sun shone from behind the mountain, throwing the valley into deep shade. Several parrots, their wings catching the last of the light, looped across the valley and disappeared into the far trees. Then he ducked his head and went under the house where Nina was clashing the buckets in an old laundry tub as she rinsed them out under a cold tap.

'So my daughter sent you to sort out the mess with the rates? That's very kind of you. But now I owe you the money. I hope you're not in a hurry for it. It's going to take me years to pay it back.' Nina wiped the buckets with a bit of cloth and stored them under the tub, then wiped her hands on the back of her skirt. 'Come on upstairs and I'll put the kettle on.'

John smiled. 'I don't think you need to worry about that. You could pay me back ten times over and not even notice the difference. That's what I've come up here to tell you.'

Nina took a step backwards. She put her hands behind her and gripped the edge of the laundry tub. 'I don't know who you've been talking to, Mr O'Shea, but I think you've made a mistake. I don't have any money at all.'

'No mistake, I assure you. I've been in Ney Creek all day looking at Mr Mander's papers. Including his will.'

'Cliff's will? Why on earth did Cliff make a will? He didn't have anything to leave.'

John was becoming annoyed. This was hardly the welcome he had envisaged for his precious news.

'Mrs Flowers, I went to the Council offices in Ney Creek today. Cliff owned all this land. Forty-odd acres. A row of shops in town. A couple of acres by the river. And now you do. Cliff left everything to you.'

Nina shook her head. 'I don't believe it.' She led the way up the back stairs and went through the open door into a large kitchen, gloomy in the half-light of evening. She indicated one of the old wooden chairs set around the big wooden table. 'Sit down, Mr O'Shea.'

John sat down and spread his hands out on the scratched surface of the table. 'But surely you must have realised the land belonged to somebody?'

Nina shook her head. 'I didn't think anyone owned it. I mean, who'd want to? Except for a mob of hippies who wanted something for nothing.'

She filled an old black kettle at the tap over the sink and plonked it onto the top of the stove, grabbed a cloth and reached down to throw a couple of logs through a creaking metal door.

'There's miles and miles of it unused. And it was in a dreadful mess in the beginning. The paddocks...' She waved her hand in the direction of the dark fields. '... they don't look much good now, I know, but they were ten times worse when we first arrived. Would have been rainforest, if it hadn't been for the lantana. We practically had to tunnel our way to the house.' She reached up and took cups out of a cupboard and put them onto the table. 'And it was a wreck, too. All the stumps were rotten. And the roof leaked. Hardly what you'd call a desirable property.'

'So you didn't know anything about what Cliff owned?'

Nina turned from the table to attend to the kettle which was boiling fiercely. 'What he stood up in. The ute. And a watch. A good one. But he only ever wore it when he went to Brisbane. He was involved in some group. A support group for veterans who couldn't cope. He'd been in Vietnam, see? He used to go up to town once or twice a year. Strap on that watch of his, drive away, come back a couple of days later and take his watch off. Lie on the bed.' She shrugged. 'I never knew what he did while he was away. He didn't want to talk about it. He went to that big march in Sydney how long ago? Five, six years? Went on the bus. Two days in bed when he got back.'

Nina brought the pot of tea to the table, dipped a jug into a cloth-covered bucket standing on the draining board and reached into a box under the sink for a small green bush lemon that she chopped into slices and put onto an old saucer.

'There's only goat's milk. And no sugar, so don't ask for it.'

'I'll have lemon.'

Nina picked up the tea pot and swirled it gently in her hands. She poured the tea and pushed John's cup towards him across the table. 'You still haven't told me what this is all about, Mr ...'

'John. Call me John.' He reached for the cup. 'Your daughter wrote to me. Or rather that fellow she's living with did. A nice bloke, that. I liked him. She wanted money for the baby. I suppose she knew there was no point writing to Michael ...'

'Michael?'

'My son.'

'And he has no money?'

'Oh, he has money all right. But it all comes from me.' John picked up a slice of lemon between thumb and finger and dropped it into the hot tea. 'I pay him to stay away, if you want the truth. He upsets my wife. Who is not his mother.' And then, in response to the look on Nina's face. 'He did a good job of upsetting his own mother, too, so I wouldn't waste your sympathy, if I were you.'

'So what happened?' asked Nina. 'With Collette, I mean?'

'I went to see her. By the time I got there, she'd changed her mind. She asked if I could fix up your problem with the rates instead. I'm a lawyer, you see. I suppose she thought I'd know what to do, though cottage conveyancing is more my wife's line than mine.'

'So how did you do it? I went down there myself and they never told me a thing.'

John reached into his jacket pocket and pulled out one of his business cards which he flipped between his fingers.

'One of these and a winning smile is all you need.' He grinned. 'But seriously, it wasn't that difficult. It's the sort of thing I do every day in court. Take a guess, present it as fact and then wait for corroboration or contradiction. Of course, it was hardly fair in a little place like Ney Creek. They were falling over themselves to tell me what they knew.'

'So you went in the council offices and showed them your card. Then what happened?'

John shook his head. 'I didn't show them my card to begin

84

with. I asked for a rates search which anybody can do. They were going to sell Hill End to a developer, did you know that?'

'I had some idea.'

'I asked the council bloke why he hadn't sent out notices and he said he'd sent them to Cliff's business address which I guessed was the bank across the road.'

'How did you work that one out?'

'The bank was one of Cliff's tenants so I thought there was some logic in him giving them his business. So I suggested it. And he confirmed it. He wasn't a very clever man.'

Nina smiled. 'So then you went across to the bank and asked for Cliff s papers?'

John sipped his tea carefully. Put the cup down on the table. 'Exactly right. Even so, I wasn't prepared for what I found. When I tell you, you'll understand why I was so surprised you knew nothing about it.'

'Tell me what?'

'Cliff had an investment portfolio valued somewhere in the region of half a million dollars. As well as the land and the shops.'

'Half a million dollars?' Nina picked up the tea pot and swirled it vigorously. 'But where the hell did Cliff get that kind of money?'

'You tell me.'

'I haven't the faintest idea.' Nina plonked the tea pot on the table. She turned and lit the lamp, setting the shadows jumping and banishing what was left of the daylight beyond the open windows. As if on cue the sound of the cicadas swelled to a shrill chorus. 'I've got a bottle of wine somewhere. Have a glass with me.'

'No, I'd better go.' John stood up and patted his pockets, looking for keys. 'I want to drive back to Brisbane tonight. My wife's expecting me.

'But you can't just go. Come in here and drop a bombshell like that and then just leave. What am supposed to do now? About the money? About Hill End? I can't deal with it. I wouldn't know where to begin.'

'Look, Nina, I've done what I said I'd do. The farm's yours now. You don't have to worry about it any more.'

'Yes, and I'm grateful. Of course I am.'

'Then I don't see what else I can do for you. If it's free financial advice you're after, you're looking at the wrong man.'

Nina shook her head. 'I don't think advice would do me much good. Not tonight. I just need someone to talk to. Please?'

'Well, okay, then. Just one glass. I think we could both do with it.'

Nina got up from the table and, leaving the circle of lamplight, retreated into the gloom. She returned with a slim green bottle which she handed to John while she rummaged in a drawer for a corkscrew.

'It's peapod. Almost the last of it. Only three bottles left.' She grinned. 'I often wondered what would happen when it ran out. I suppose I can afford to buy some more now, can't I?

John pulled the cork and poured the pale green liquid. They touched glasses and drank a toast. 'To you,' he said. 'The wealthy Mrs Flowers.'

'To Cliff,' said Nina. 'I suppose it's him we ought to be drinking to.'

John sipped the wine, then swallowed cautiously. It tasted sweet enough but with a dry aftertaste that was not too bad after several mouthfuls What they would call a crisp finish in wine-tasting circles. The alcohol hit his tired brain like a sledgehammer.

Nina got to her feet. 'I'll get us something to eat.'

John poured himself a refill and sat watching the woman busy around the kitchen. The end of a loaf cut into thick slices. Some sort of soft white cheese on an old saucer. A handful of small red tomatoes, smelling of childhood.

'There's a bunch of bananas hanging in the front room,' she said. 'Go and get some, will you?'

John got up stiffly and, following Nina's directions, went out of the door into a long hall. The first door he opened was to a bedroom with curtains moving softly in the breeze from an open window and the bed hung with the ghostly shape of a mosquito net.

Across the hall, an empty room, smelling dusty and unused, the bananas a black shape like a hanged man. They felt hard and cold under his fingers and he grabbed at them, suddenly afraid.

Back in the kitchen he presented the bananas to Nina.

'But they're green. Why didn't you get ripe ones?'

'I didn't know which ones they were. I couldn't see.'

'Ripe ones at the top. They always ripen from the top down. Surely you know that? Even a fancy lawyer like you.' She handed him another bottle of the green wine. 'Open this, then. You can do that, I dare say.'

They ate in silence. John was hungry, cramming the good food on top of the remains of his lunchtime junk. When they had finished eating Nina unhooked the lamp and led the way along the hall.

'Come and sit outside while we finish our wine.'

Outside, the wide veranda was bathed in bright silver light from a full moon riding in a velvety summer sky. So bright was the moon that it cast long black shadows on the ground and showed the colour of the leaves hanging motionless on the tall gums that stood near the house. Lightning flickered silently in the fringe of clouds glowing white beyond the swell of the far hillside.

There were two low-slung canvas chairs standing on the warm timber floor. Nina put the lamp between the two chairs where it shone a sullen gold against the stronger challenge of the moon.

'What happens now?'

Ever since his first sip of wine and the realisation that he was not going home that night, John's thoughts had been moving steadily in the direction of Nina's bed, half-glimpsed through the open doorway, and for a moment he wondered if she had read his mind.

She leaned forward and poured the last of the wine into his glass. 'With Cliff's papers,' she said. 'Won't I have to do something with them?'

'Look, don't worry about it. I'll find someone to handle the estate for you. I'll take you into town first thing in the morning to pick up the boxes from the bank.'

'It's very kind of you.'
'Not in the least.'

Later in the night Nina was woken by a strong cool wind blowing through the open window of her bedroom. She lay still listening to the steady breathing of the man next to her and the sound of thunder shuddering in the warm air. Quietly she left the bed, shivering as she wrapped an old cotton blanket around her bare shoulders.

'Where are you going?' John's voice was muffled by sleep.

'I have to check the shed. I don't remember fastening the latch.'

As Nina walked down the hill the storm was all around her, beating its soft wings against her head, while the clouds streamed out towards the high peak of the mountain beyond the valley. Thunder growled. The little dog walked as close to Nina's feet as she could, whining softly in her throat.

Nina checked the latch, murmuring gentle words to the animal shifting inside. Then she stood for a while, feeling the first heavy drops of rain on her face. She was aware of the warm breast of the hill beneath her naked feet. Her hill. Her land. It felt good.

TEN

By eleven o'clock the following morning, the freshness brought by the storm had gone, replaced by an oppressive heat. Nina and John were sitting on the verandah of the Ney Creek hotel drinking beer, the boxes from the bank on the floor by John's chair. Nina was enjoying herself. Ney Creek was a very different place in the company of someone like John O'Shea.

First the journey into town in John's car, the air-conditioning cocooning her from the dust and heat of the road. Then the interview at the bank where it appeared she was now a valued customer. Offers of help and assistance from a young man with cheerful eyes who seemed somehow to be best friends with John.

And now, sitting in the black shade of the pub verandah, with the crisp, cold beer clearing the last of the wine-induced fog from her brain, enjoying the feeling of warmth in a place where nothing warm had been for a long, long time. It had been good sex in spite of - or perhaps because of - the wine they had drunk and because of rather than in spite of the old bed they had slept in which had made it impossible for them to be anything other than together. She had woken in the night and felt the length of a man's body against her own and realised how much she had missed it.

She watched John reach down into one of the boxes by his chair and extract several pieces of paper which he laid out carefully on the table in front of him. He was neat. Nina had noticed it last night. Folding his trousers by the creases and looking around the bedroom for a chair to put them on. Laying the trousers on the floor when a chair was not to be found, and the rest of his clothes folded on top of them. He had a good body, too, once everything was off. Hard to believe he was the father of a grown son. She looked at his fine, long-fingered hands smoothing out the papers on the table and felt a twinge of desire, remembering where they had been the night before.

There had been that cruise she went on when she was seventeen. What made her think of that? The same throb of remembered pleasure. The cold beer chasing away last night's hangover. It was where she met Collette's father. She remembered the last night, staying up until dawn to watch the moonlight on the water as the ship negotiated Moreton Bay, picking up the beacons into the river just as the sun began to lighten the sky

'This is Cliff's will.' John's voice, harsh against her thoughts. 'It's all fairly straightforward. Is there anything you don't understand?'

Nina shook her head.

'And you're happy for me to hand it over to a solicitor in town? I don't think there'll be any difficulty obtaining probate.'

'Yes, that's fine.'

'Well, that's it then. You're a wealthy woman. Now all you have to do is decide what you're going to do with it.'

'What do you mean?'

John rubbed the back of his neck. He hadn't scrubbed up all that well this morning, which was unusual for him, and that whisky he'd had in the bar while he spoke to his wife on the telephone probably hadn't helped.

'Well, first of all you'll have to manage it. Or get someone to manage it for you. A portfolio like that won't look after itself. Or you could think of another way of investing the money. For instance, you could put some of it into Hill End.'

'Hill End? I suppose the house could do with a lick of paint.'

'I wasn't thinking of a lick of paint. Look, Nina, Hill End is a beautiful place. Hill End with a bit of money spent on it would be magnificent. Open it up for visitors. That's what I'd do. Tourism's the place to put your money these days. It'd give you a better return than some of the stuff Cliff invested in.' He pulled a face. 'Distinctly eighties, a lot of it.'

'But I wouldn't know where to begin.'

But John had lost interest. What I really need is a good shit, he thought to himself, but I'm going to have to wait until I get back to the city because I have no desire to submit myself to Nina's sawdust and shovel arrangement no matter how desperate I am. You'd think Cliff would have done at least that much and put in decent plumbing. A necessity of life, if ever there was one. He swallowed the last of his beer.

'Think about it,' he said, getting to his feet. 'And talk to Collette. That's all you need to do for the time being. Now, are you ready to go?' He bent to pick up the boxes from the floor and turned to carry them to the car. 'So, how do you feel? Has it sunk in yet?'

Nina walked around to the side of the car, the silver bells on her skirt chiming softly, and waited for John to open the door for her. 'I'm getting used to it,' she said, seating herself on the soft upholstery.

They sat in silence until the car was clear of the town and John was enjoying the challenge of the narrow road leading up to the farm.

'The only thing I can't understand is why he didn't tell you,' he said finally.

'He must have intended to. He would have known well enough that I wouldn't go down to Ney Creek and ask. I mean, why would I?'

'Perhaps he wondered how you'd take it. Finding out about the money. I mean, how do you feel, Nina? Don't you feel cheated.'

'Why should I feel cheated?'

'Look at the way you live. And all that money in the bank. Think what you could have had all these years. I know I'd be feeling pretty pissed off, if it was me.'

She shrugged. 'We had a good life. What difference would the money have made?'

All the difference in the world, thought John, who had read Cliff's books of accounts, because without it the silly cow wouldn't be at Hill End at all, even hanging on by the bare threads as she was doing now. He had a growing respect for the unknown Clifford Mander who, despite his hippy aspirations, had understood the value of money.

At the house Nina said, 'Are you going to stay and eat?'

John scrambled nimbly out of the car and stood on the dusty track, struck by the sudden heat from the white-hot midday sky

'No, I can't. I rang my wife. She's expecting me.'

'Cup of tea then?'

'Only if it's quick.'

John sat down on the bottom step, feeling the heat seeping into his body. The sun-struck land lay before him, the trees panting in circles of shade. He remembered what it had been like in the early morning when back pain had forced him from Nina's bed and he had sat on the veranda and watched the sun come up, a whisper of light through the white mist left over from last night's storm, the drops of water in the trees sparkling like jewels laid out for his pleasure. I'm going to have some of this, he thought, and felt an answering tightness in his loins. For John O'Shea the prospect of making money was as enticing as the prospect of making love. And as easy to do, he thought, that was the thing. A piece of piss.

Nina came down the steps carrying two mugs.

'You know I'll help, don't you,' said John, reaching up to take his tea. 'Whatever you decide to do.'

And was rewarded with a grateful smile.

He drank the scalding tea, handed Nina his empty mug and kissed her briefly.

'Look, I've got to go. I'll talk to you soon.'

John opened his car door and smelled the cool, slightly metallic odour of the air conditioning, mingled with the smell of yesterday's chips and the musty perfume from the old boxes piled up on the back seat. He felt his mind leap ahead up the highway towards his Brisbane office and the home where Naomi waited with his little kids. He looked up to where Nina stood on the steps, the empty mugs clutched in her hands. Behind her the old unpainted house creaked in the heat. And all around the loud scream of cicadas in the hot trees.

It was like winning lotto.

Nina listened to the sound of the car fading into the distance and then went back into the house. She prepared dough for bread and set it by the stove to rise. She boiled the kettle and made another pot of tea. Then, ignoring the bawling of the unmilked goat, she sat at the table and pulled the first of the boxes towards her. John had taken the share certificates, bank statements and books of account to Brisbane with him and had left behind all Cliff s personal papers which filled two of the cardboard document boxes to overflowing. It took her several hours to work her way through the boxes but finally she had everything piled on the table in some sort of order. The last thing she found was a blurred black and white photograph, fading to brown, showing a sturdy child about ten years old wearing baggy knee-length shorts and a checked shirt. He had a long stick in one hand, held upright like a spear. The other hand was resting on the head of a disreputable dog sitting to attention by his side. Nina propped the photograph up against the milk jug and went out to milk the goat.

Cliff's father had won the Golden Casket when Cliff was eight years old. The family moved to a leafy little side street in Ekibin, into a house which represented all Cliff's mother's hopes and dreams. For Cliff's father it was a different story. The old man just thought that rent was wasted money and if there was one thing he hated doing it was wasting money. The big win didn't alter his opinion. Hold on to it all the tighter, when you've got a bit, that's what he reckoned.

Once he'd bought the house, old man Mander closed the lid on his treasure box. He told his wife Rita to forget about a car or a holiday or all the fancy furniture she kept looking at in Tritton's window. He put his money into the bank and carried on going to work. The only thing he did differently was to increase the housekeeping money he gave to his wife. He thought a rich man like him should be able to eat steak every night of the week, if he wanted to. Rita promptly gave up her part time job in the Greek milk bar at Chardon's

Corner, which left Cliff to the tender mercies of Rita Mander and her mother, Cliff's granny - two women whose sole mission in life was to spoil him rotten.

Cliff, who was never more than an average student and hopeless at sport, had trouble fitting in at his new school. He became something of a loner, spending time in his bedroom attending to his collections – insects, stones, bottle-tops, in fact anything he could find that didn't cost any money - or out in the back yard playing with an old grey dog he'd found when he was out on his paper round.

In 1969 he turned eighteen and in the following March he was picked out of the birthday ballots for conscription to Vietnam. The old man went to the pub and bought a round of drinks. Like father, like son he said, having spent his own war guarding Italian internees on the chilly western plains of New South Wales. This was where he had met young Rita, seventeen years old and working in the canteen. He had shagged her every Saturday night for the duration and Wednesdays, too, if her mother went to the pictures. Not bad going, he'd always thought, with a camp full of Italians for her to choose from.

Cliff had to go to Townsville to do his basic training before they sent him overseas, and Granny and Rita went to Roma Street station to see him off. After Cliff's train left, Granny took Rita to the Criterion Hotel in George Street and poured a few gins into her to cheer her up. When old man Mander came home for his tea the pair of them were lying on top of their beds in their petticoats, snoring their head off.

Cliff got some R & R half way through his tour of duty so he came home to see his mum, hitching a ride on an American transport plane with a group of GIs eager for a few days relaxation with the Brisbane ladies. He'd put on a lot of weight while he'd been away. A huge man, he was now. A huge man with a boy's face. Sitting at the kitchen table drinking beer with his hand on the head of the old dog who sat next to him watching him carefully with his red, rheumy eyes. But there was something hard about him, too. Something that hadn't been there before. He wore his army greens. Black boots. A webbing belt. He had a gun with him, too. He put it on the table to show Rita. A mean little thing with a clip of bullets. He said he carried it everywhere. He didn't feel safe in Brisbane. It was too quiet. Not enough crowds. And all those faces looking at him.

It was August and on the Show Day Wednesday he went drinking with the Yanks at the Belle Vue Hotel in Queen Street, out on the balcony overlooking the Post Office. All the country people were down for the Show. White shirts and country hats. Moleskin trousers. Yuppies wear them now but in those days you could tell the farmers a mile off. They used to squat down with their backs to the buildings, resting on one heel, and roll themselves a smoke. Cliff thought they were beggars crouched on the corners, like the ones in Saigon. He went and spoke to one of them. Tried to give him money for beer. Would have got his head punched in, only he was so big. Poor Cliff, blundering around the streets of Brisbane with a loaded pistol in his pocket, looking for trouble that wasn't there. In the end he was glad to go back.

By the time Cliff finished his tour in Vietnam, his father had retired from work and was occupying himself managing his investments. There was a lot of money to be made in speculative mining stock and Mr. Mander didn't trust anyone else to do it properly. It was unfortunate for Cliff and his mother that the old man was home all day at a time when the need to give and receive love was so strong in both their hearts. To begin with, all Cliff wanted to do was sleep during the day and then go out after tea to drink beer with his mates. After a month or so, the old man started making noises about getting a job. He told Rita not to give Cliff any money and was able to enforce the rule because he had taken charge of the purse strings to the extent that Rita seldom had more than a few dollars to call her own. But she had her stash. Like most women of her generation she had always put a bit by against hard times. Not that Rita had ever needed to use it. Old man Mander had always been a good provider, and winning the Casket meant Rita would never have to worry about money again. But there it was. A tidy sum hidden away in a cocoa tin at the back of the chook-house. And, although Mr Mander knew well enough that Cliff was getting his beer money off his mother, he never did figure out how she did it.

Cliff and his mates had an office at the top of the old Trades Hall building in Upper Edward Street. They were all Vietnam veterans and were suppose to be organising some sort of a committee to coordinate aid for those that needed it. Rita went up there once to find him. He hadn't been home for three days and she was worried about him. It was a hot day. Stinking hot with a clear blue sky. Brisbane was full of traffic, swirling down the hill from Wickham Terrace and leaving a trail of fumes behind as it went. Cliff's office was at the top of steep, disinfectant-smelling stairs. The door was open. Brown carpet on the floor. A telephone sitting on the carpet. A large fridge with boxes of beer piled next to it. The window was open, spilling hot air into the room. Outside the window there was a metal fire-escape and, at the top of the fire-escape, the noise of a radio, very loud.

Rita was not keen on heights and she was a woman well into her fifties so it took all her courage to climb out of that window. It felt like she was at the top of the world with the whole of Brisbane spread out at her feet. She could see right over the tops of the trees in Albert Park. The hills beyond the city, lost in the heat haze. Roma Street railway yard down below, like a toy train set. It turned her stomach to water being up so high. But she grasped the hot metal of the handrail and climbed up steadily, her handbag looped carefully over one arm. At the top was a flat roof surrounded by a low parapet. Boiling hot. Cliff and a couple of his mates flat on their backs staring at the sky. Loud music on the radio. Bottles of beer standing around.

Cliff made his mother sit down. Offered her a beer. She wrapped her lips around the top of the bottle and tipped the bitter, astringent liquid into her mouth. Alcohol and strong sunlight wrought their effects on a head not used to either. She felt her eye lids drooping. Felt the rough stone of the parapet through the thin fabric of her summer frock.

Cliff said it reminded them of Vietnam, lying on the roof. There was a hill behind the camp. Nothing on it but bare dirt.

They used to go up there at night and smoke dope. Listen to music on this huge radio they'd bought from the US army store and watch the fire-fights in the distance. Lie on their backs and watch the stars and wonder which of their mates was going to come home with his belly full of shrapnel or his knackers blown off from stepping on a mine. Sorry, Mum. It was only the helicopters they missed. The sound of helicopters and the smell of mud and diesel and beer and chemicals. That's what the place smelled like, no joke.

'Not like here,' growled one of the other men, grinning at Rita with a mouth full of broken teeth. 'You land in Brisbane and all you can smell is frangipani. What sort of a place smells of fucking frangipani?'

Rita stayed all afternoon listening to Cliff and his mates talking. For her it was the most precious experience of her life. And the most frightening. It made her realise at last how far her child had gone from her and why he was never coming back.

In 1976 Cliff's parents were killed in an accident. Old man Mander had finally bought a car, just some old thing to run around in and they were on Ipswich Road going to the shops when they were collected by a truck which had run a red light. After the funeral, neighbours and friends went back to the house for sandwiches and cake. It was the middle of the week so it was very much a ladies' day with the priest and Cliff the only males represented. With the kitchen full of people scoffing food and spilling cake crumbs on the floor, Cliff went out onto the back stairs. It was a hot day but cooler out there with the bay breeze just beginning to blow. He pulled the tab off a can of beer and leaned on the railings, looking out at the garden. At the banana trees and the heap of grass clippings and the old, unpainted, falling-down fence half buried under a choko vine. At the Hill's hoist, hung with plastic pegs, and the narrow cracked concrete path leading to the place where the dunny used to be before Clem Jones sewered Brisbane. And, beyond, to the bit of grass where he used to play and the creek, now no more than a concrete drain, and the new freeway, full of the murmur of traffic, striding on colossal legs across his childhood world. For a long while he stood there sucking the beer and listening to the voices inside the house. He had been to see the solicitor the day before and knew he was a wealthy man. A wealthy man with no needs other than a cold beer, a plentiful supply of hash and somewhere quiet to live. And his mother. Especially his mother. Which was the one thing his money couldn't buy.

He sold the Ekibin house, gave the furniture to the Salvation Army and bought Hill End, sight unseen, when it was auctioned off as part of a deceased estate. Then he drove south in his new ute with his belongings in the back and a brand new cattle dog pup squirming in a blanket-lined box on the seat by his side.

Which is more or less where I come in, thought Nina, with her head resting on the goat's warm flank and her hands busy stripping milk from the animal's distended udder. Two years later, three months pregnant with her holiday souvenir, she had run away from home a couple of days ahead of being thrown out by her father. She'd hitched a ride with a truck driver who'd made it clear he'd want a reward for his efforts, and jumped out of the truck in Ney Creek when he stopped for a leak. Cliff was parked on the other side of the road, loading sacks of feed into the back of the ute. He picked her up off the bitumen, threw her bag in the back, opened the passenger door for her to climb in and took her home to Hill End.

And, when she asked herself why she had gone with him, she could never find a satisfactory answer. As to why she stayed, she never knew whether it was simply because she had nowhere else to go or because she found something at Hill End, something that was more than the freedom it offered and the joint passed around in the peace of late afternoon.

After all, it was hard work, back-breaking work, clearing stones by hand from the paddocks and then tending plants that wilted constantly in the rocky ground. Chopping wood and hauling water from the creek. Fighting the flying foxes for the precious bunches of bananas, and the dingoes for the chooks. Nina remembered Cliff sitting at the top of the back stairs in the cool of the evening with his big hands caressing the rifle across his knees, smoking peacefully and waiting for a particular dog to walk up the hill in search of his supper.

Twelve months after Collette was born Nina fell pregnant again. It wasn't an easy pregnancy and she nearly lost the baby a couple of times. In the end she was admitted to the hospital in Black Rock. They were going to send her to Brisbane only she went into labour unexpectedly very early one morning. The child did not live. The matron told Nina as kindly as she could that her baby had been grossly deformed. Could never have lived any sort of normal life. She had been matron at the hospital in Narrabri, in the heart of cotton country, before she came to Black Rock, and she had seen many like it. More than she cared to think about. She told Nina to go home and try again.

But as soon as Nina was back home, Cliff told her he was going to Brisbane to get himself fixed up. This was at the time that the veterans in America were trying to get evidence to link Agent Orange to birth defects and, through his involvement with the local veterans, Cliff had found himself privy to some highly sensitive material that had come into the hands of the US veterans from sympathetic sources at the very top of their federal administration. Cliff's army career had consisted of loading things on and off aircraft. Helicopters out to the fire bases with ammo and supplies. Planes with various types of missiles. And, of course, Agent Orange. He never took any precautions. None of them did. So far as they were concerned, the stuff was for taking leaves off trees. They never imagined it could be harmful to humans. Cliff told Nina they used to get covered with the stuff. Sit on half-empty barrels having smoko. Sit in the mess after work drinking beer before they had a shower. Never thought anything about it until he started getting involved with the veterans. But, when that baby was born, he knew straight away what had caused it.

Nina remembered the night he came home from Brisbane. She had sat up late waiting for him after the others had gone to bed. Had heard the particular sound of his ute as he crossed the old wooden bridge and gunned it up the slope. Had the kettle boiling for tea by the time he walked into the kitchen. Cliff had sat down at the table and rested his head in his hands. Accepted the tea without speaking. Gulped it down and pushed his mug across the table for more. Finally he spoke.

'There was this bloke. I remember unloading him off the helicopter. Only a young fellow. He'd set off a booby trap out on patrol. Came in with his legs hanging off and nothing but a bit of bloody rag stuffed between them. And he was crying. He was pumped up with painkillers so he wasn't feeling anything. But he knew what had happened to him. And he was crying. Just quietly. Whimpering like a little kid. It would have been better somehow if he had been screaming. Or … or swearing. I could have put up with that. I felt sorry for him, the poor bastard. I mean, who wouldn't? But I never knew how he felt. Not really.' And he looked up into Nina's face. 'Now I do. Because it's happened to me. What happened to him. It's happened to me.'

ELEVEN

By the middle of May the weather had cooled down and Frank was ready to make a start on the extensions to the shack. The timber was delivered, great long bales of it which killed the grass where it lay and created an obstacle course for Collette on her daily journeys to the washing line and the tin shed beyond that housed their bathroom. Frank went into town and bought several boxes of nails. Then, with a pencil tucked behind one ear, and whistling cheerfully, he set to work. Collette became accustomed to the noise of the power saw and the regular clunk, clunk of an old cement mixer that Frank had acquired from a bloke in the pub. Ian, just standing, spent his waking days hanging over the wooden barrier which Frank had built across the back door.

Soon the back of the house was a network of posts and joists and timber frames with Frank in the middle like a great scrawny monkey, with his mouth full of nails or squatting down to read his plans, hastily scribbled the night before. Every now and again he would call Collette to him. 'Where do you want a window?' Or listen carefully while she, who had never had one before, explained to him why the bathroom on his plans was far too small.

'I'll get the cat, if you like,' she said aggressively. 'And swing it around Then you'll see.'

Frank had chosen to build in hardwood - twice the price of plantation pine and three times as hard to build with - but he had no faith in anything less to withstand the harsh conditions so close to the sea.

'Wood doesn't rust, does it?' asked Collette, when he tried to explain his reasoning.

But Frank liked the feel of this wood, the colour of it freshly-cut, and the smell of it. He liked the weight of it as he heaved it into position.

'Get a cyclone through here and this won't budge.' he said, slapping his hand against his latest upright, and Collette laughed.

'The front will,' she said. 'Never mind a cyclone. A bit of a puff and it'll go.'

'Well, we'll know where to go when it blows, won't we?' said Frank. 'Now, hand me a nail, girl, and stop your nattering.'

To begin with Collette had been amused by the large tin of thick red engine grease into which Frank dunked the nails before hammering them into place. He said that it made the nails easier to drive into the wood. Collette said he was as bad as the baby and how was she supposed to get the oil stains off the back of his shorts? However now she crouched down and dunked the nails for him and handed them to him one by one as his big bony hand came down to take them.

This was what they were doing when Michael O'Shea came up from the beach and heard the sound of hammering coming from the house. He walked through the gap in the greenery and into the warm peace of the garden. In the middle of the circle of untidy bush grass there was an old cane chair with a patchwork cushion and a long table made out of rough timber. On the table a large cat lay sleeping half upside down in a patch of sunshine. A pair of magpies walked around the edge of the garden in and out of the shade, poking for insects. There was a child's swing made out of an old tyre hanging from a tree near the house. Underneath it a blue plastic elephant with a well-chewed trunk lay abandoned in the dirt.

Through the veranda where Collette's collection of sarongs hung from the ceiling in dusty spirals. Into the cool gloomy kitchen, heat puffing from an old wood stove in an alcove on the far side, the remains of a meal on the table, an easel set up next to the sink where it caught the light from the window, and a plump blond baby in a grubby towelling all-in-one and an expensive hand-knitted cardigan sitting on the floor, playing with a saucepan and a collection of timber off-cuts sanded smooth.

The child looked up. Smiled. Offered his father a piece of wood held in a damp hand. Watched him carefully as he stepped up to the wooden barrier across the door and peered out. Among the mess of timber, Collette reached up and handed Frank a nail. Michael didn't need to hear them speak or see them touch but had only to observe the look that passed between them to know that things had changed. And what he had come for he couldn't have. The baby decided he was frightened and yelled suddenly and loudly. Collette and Frank looked up. It was a while before anyone spoke.

Frank was the first to recover. 'Hullo there, young man.' He wiped his hands on the back of his shorts and began to make his way out of the mess of timbers, moving with the trained grace of an actor which sat oddly with his general appearance. He reached the door and offered Michael his hand. Then he paused, turned it palm-up and inspected it closely for a long moment before wiping it again on the seat of his pants. The two shook hands.

'Put the kettle on, will you?' Frank said to Collette who had not yet moved. 'Did you come along the beach? Not so pleasant today. I was out earlier on.' Still talking, the older man stepped over the wooden barrier across the door and led Michael into the kitchen. 'Sit down, lad. Sit down.'

Frank sprawled in the old armchair by the side of the stove and reached for his pouch of tobacco. The baby, abandoned by the door, crawled rapidly to the chair and pulled himself upright against Frank's legs, his head swivelling around anxiously to keep the stranger in view. Frank reached down and pulled the baby onto his knee, wrapped one arm around him and proceeded to roll himself a smoke, turning his head to prevent the baby from snatching the small square of paper that he had stuck to his bottom lip, obviously an old game.

Michael perched himself on one of the old kitchen chairs around the table and contemplated his son. The child was sturdy, with his mother's pale hair and fine skin. On his cheeks were two bright circles of colour caused by the imminent arrival of new teeth. His eyes were fixed steadily on Michael's face.

Collette came into the kitchen, filled the kettle at the sink and thumped it onto the stove. She snatched the baby from Frank's knee, tucked him under her arm and left the room. Frank raised his eye-brows at his visitor.

'She's just gone to clean him up. She'll be back in a moment.'

When Collette had been away long enough for the kettle to boil its head off and for Frank to get up and make the tea himself, he went into the bedroom and discovered her sitting upright on the edge of the bed in the dark room staring at nothing while the baby, still grubby, fed contentedly from her breast

'Come on, Collette. Come and talk to him. It isn't me he's come to see.'

'What d'you think he wants?

Frank shrugged. 'Come and find out.'

Collette extricated the baby from under her tee-shirt, slung him over her shoulder and followed Frank out of the room.

It was an uncomfortable tea party for everyone except Ian who was put into his highchair and given a buttery crust which he succeeded in wiping all over his face and through his hair while his mother was distracted.

In the end Frank said, 'Why don't you go for a walk? It'll be nice on the beach now.' And, to Collette, 'Go on. I'll wash Ian. A nice clean bath in the sink, my lad!' he said to the baby, turning his back.

Collette followed Michael out of the house and onto the beach. 'I'm always going for walks with you people,' she said crossly, kicking the dry sand and feeling it sting against her legs as the wind picked it up and flung it back. 'First your dad. Now you.'

'I heard.'

They walked down onto the wet sand and set off towards the Rock with the stiff afternoon breeze at their backs. Despite Frank's prediction, it was not particularly nice on the beach, the strength already fading from the sun as the day drew to a close. Collette walked quickly and said nothing, feeling the chill of the damp sand against her bare feet.

'What's up, Collette?' Michael reached out his hand to grab her arm. 'Come on, slow down.'

'What do you want, Michael?'

'Nothing. I've just come to see you and the baby. Nothing wrong with that, is there?'

'What was wrong with before?'

'Be reasonable, Collette. I didn't know before. Why didn't you tell me?'

'If you'd come to see me you'd have found out for yourself.'

'I rang the caravan park. They didn't know where you'd gone.'

The words hung between them. Collette thought he was probably lying.

'Well, now you know. What are you going to do about it?'

'I'm not going to do anything. I just wanted to see him.' Michael gripped Collette's arm and swung her around to face him. 'Why did you tell my father about Ian? My father?'

Collette wriggled to get free. 'It was Frank's idea. It had nothing to do with me.'

'But what about me, Collette? Didn't you think how I'd feel?'

'I'd sort of forgotten about you by then.' She stared up at him. 'Look, Michael, we had fun, okay? But it wasn't anything real. Having Ian was real. Living is real. What I'm doing now.'

'I thought you loved me.'

'I did.'

'You're not even wearing the ear rings I bought you.'

Collette reached up and touched the thin silver wire looped through her ear.

'Jim gave me these.'

'Jim? Who's Jim?'

'He isn't anybody. He just gives me things sometimes, that's all.'

'And what about Frank?'

'What about him?'

'Collette, he's old.'

Collette started walking again. 'He doesn't seem old when you're with him. He gives me books to read.'

'What's that got to do with anything?' Michael strode next to her, the cold water of the incoming tide swirling suddenly around his feet.

Collette laughed and ran up the beach away from the water. 'He keeps them under the bed. Real old ones. I don't read them all.'

They reached the shelter of the rock and the wind was gone, replaced by the chill of the afternoon shadows. They stood quite close together, a little out of breath from the walk. Collette, standing with her bare feet in wet sand, tipped up her head to see Michael's face. He was looking over her head to where the last of the sunlight shone on a procession of waves rolling slightly sideways onto the beach, pushed by the wind and the incoming tide. His face was winter-pale, a day's growth showing blue beneath his skin, his eyes like blank windows, reflecting the colour of the sea.

Finally he looked down. 'Don't be mean, Collette. You don't know what it's been like.' He grabbed her arm again. 'I've wanted you and wanted you. All this time. Don't you see?' He made another move towards her. 'And what about the baby? He's my son.'

Caught suddenly between an unexpected desire for the boy in front of her and the thought of her child, Collette felt her breasts leak milk, staining her tee-shirt and dripping down onto the skin of her stomach where the cold wind took it and made her shiver.

'Fuck off, will you?'

She took a step backwards, put her foot in a hollow in the sand, stumbled in the cold water and felt his hands grabbing at her, holding her up.

'Come on, Collette.' he said, pulling her strongly into his arms. 'I want you, don't you see? You and the baby.' Michael felt a moment of triumph. The look of desire in her eyes had not been lost on him. He looked down at her. 'I've been to Hill End.'

'What for?'

'To have a look around. I stayed there last night. Came down here this morning on the bus.'

'What's happened to your car?'

106

He grinned. 'I haven't got it any more. That's what I came to tell you.' He took her hand and began pulling her over the jumble of rocks at the back of the beach.

'Haven't got it?' Collette's feet, numb with the cold, were having difficulties negotiating the sharp rocks and she pulled her hand away sharply so that she could use it to balance herself. 'Where is it then?'

'I gave it back to my father. Not just the car. Everything.'

Standing on the sloping, rabbit-nibbled turf beyond the rocks, Michael turned around and looked down at Collette. He leaned down, held out his hand.

'Give me your hand and I'll pull you over the last bit.'

They toiled up the slope until they reached the sunshine, then Michael turned around and stood, legs apart, staring out over the sea. He looked down at Collette who was sitting hunched on the grass, her arms around her knees.

'I've left him, Collette. Told him he could stick it. Well, I didn't actually tell him. But I expect he's got the message by now.'

'Left him? What d'you mean?'

Michael crouched down. 'Not going to uni. Not living in the flat he pays for. Not driving his fucking car.'

'But why?'

'I just don't want to do it any more.'

'So what are you going to do instead?'

He grinned again. The old charm. 'Like I said. Be with you. Live at Hill End. Your mum says it's okay. We could help out ...'

'Help out? What with?'

'With this holiday camp thing she's building. You know about it, don't you?'

'Yeah, I know about it,' said Collette with disgust. 'Holiday camp!'

'What's wrong with it? I think it's a great idea.'

'Well, I don't.' She rested her chin on her knees, staring ahead. 'But it's got nothing to do with me. She can please herself what she does. She's got plenty of money. Thanks to your dad.' And then she turned her head and looked at him. For a long moment she looked at him, eye to eye. 'You are a bastard, Michael O'Shea,' she said quietly. 'A bastard. I should have known better than to listen to you.'

'Now what?'

'I just figured it out. All this shit about us living together. And here was me just starting to believe you.'

'Collette ...'

'So what am I, Michael? A free ride into Hill End? Is that the idea? I mean, you wouldn't want to piss your father off if you didn't have something else lined up, would you?'

'It isn't like that.'

Michael stood up abruptly and turned his back on Collette. He was close to crying and it was not something he was used to. The last time he had cried was when he was eight years old and his mother had loaded him onto a bus to go back to his father. Tears had done him no good then. He remembered the long journey in the dark and nobody at the other end to meet him.

He thought about the last time he'd been with his father. It had been a duty visit made to remind his father of his existence before the cheques stopped coming. Sitting at the dinner table eating Naomi's famous lasagne, hot and delicious, he had watched his father as he ate, forking up his food, snatching at it the way he always did, his knife lying idle. And Naomi sitting quietly with her blond hair tucked behind her ears, chasing morsels around her plate, having eaten more than half a meal while she was feeding her children in the kitchen.

And, while he ate, he had talked about Collette, and her mother, and Hill End as if he owned them. Just like he owned everything else. About the baby who was suddenly his grandson, and the young lass of whom he had decided to approve and to whom he had extended his favour. His largesse. Call it what you will. Easy to give when you've got the lot.

Naomi, too, had been preoccupied with the topic of Hill End. She'd mentioned Nina to Michael while he sat at the kitchen table nursing a mug of tea and watching the little kids eating their fish fingers and oven fries while the rich smell of wine and garlic filled his nostrils. Naomi had the

108

littlest child on her knee, persuading him to eat one more mouthful so he could have some ice cream for dessert. She told Michael his father had spent the night at Hill End. Wanted to know if Michael could tell her anything about this woman who had suddenly loomed into her life.

Michael wondered why she bothered getting upset about it. After all, his father had always had his bit on the side. Which was just what Naomi herself had been in the days before Michael's mother went to Sydney. And he made no secret of it. Carried condoms in his wallet, as Michael discovered on the occasions when he had been in there looking for loose change to steal. And not just the battered, tatty-round-the-edges, just-in-case condoms either but always a couple of new ones, tucked in behind the credit cards where they were easy to find. So he went through them.

And there he sat going on and on about Hill End, and Nina, and how he'd saved her from the brink of disaster. And provided for Collette and the child into the bargain. Gulping at the red wine and getting more and more loquacious, more pleased with himself, as if he were the best bloke who had ever lived instead of what he was. A grabber. A user. A thrower away.

Michael had walked out. Gone back to the flat. Packed a bag with a few clothes and his precious CD collection. Locked the door. Posted the key into the letter box out front. Driven the car to his father's house. Parked it in the driveway. Tossed the keys into the bushes on his way out. Walked down the road with his bag heavy on his shoulder and the cool night wind drying the sweat between his shoulder blades. Heading south as if he'd known all along that was what he was going to do.

Now he wiped his face with the flat of his hand. Crouched down beside Collette. 'Just tell me. Do you want to come with me or not? I don't care what you think. It's not true but I don't care.'

She turned her face and looked at him. 'No, I don't want to come with you, Michael. Get it? I don't want to come with you and I don't want to live at Hill End. I'm staying here with Frank.'

He grinned suddenly, the sort of grin that melted girls' hearts routinely. 'Nothing I can do to change your mind?'

Collette grinned back. 'No.' And then, 'What are you going to do now?'

'I'm going back to Hill End. I told you. Your mum needs a hand.'

Collette stood up. Brushed the dry grass from the back of her shorts. 'See you around then.'

And walked away. Left him standing. An odd feeling. To be alone with his long black shadow in front of him and the wind whistling through the tawny grass and the great ocean at his feet. And the girl walking away. Hurrying away. An odd feeling indeed. But not bad. Not as bad as he thought it would be. Michael turned and began walking towards the town.

TWELVE

John O'Shea twitched his foot on the accelerator pedal and felt the big car lift underneath him as it mounted the first steep hill out of Ney Creek. It was a feeling that never failed to satisfy him, particularly on an early spring day with the air-conditioning full on and the stereo turned up loud. He grinned to himself and lifted one hand to smooth his hair.

Things were going well. Australia was lifting out of a period of depression and John had renegotiated Nina's portfolio of term deposits to take advantage of the rising interest rates. There was nothing like a swag of money to make financial institutions sit up and take notice. Or an investment adviser whose son you'd helped avoid a conviction for dangerous driving only the previous year. At the thought of his friend's son, John's good mood evaporated. He hadn't seen Michael for six months.

He drove the car through the gates into Hill End and felt his spirits lift. The old wooden stand had been demolished and the gateposts removed to widen the entrance. Either side of the gate was a decorative plank fence with the name 'Hill End Farm' picked out in green paint. Narrow bark gardens had been planted with grevilleas which were in full crimson bloom. The old dusty track had been graded and sealed with crushed gravel and led to a house that no longer looked like an old animal crouched in the dirt. A new tin roof and cream paint on the walls had done wonders for the old place.

John parked his car under the house next to Nina's ute and walked out into the sunshine. He stretched until he heard the bones crack in his back, then walked around the side of the house, past the old vegetable garden where no chooks scratched and down the hill. There had been no rain during winter and the paddock was dry. Fine dust rose in clouds beneath his feet. Along the fence on one side of the paddock grey electrical cords hung in long loops with every now and then a loose knot where plug met plug. He looked down the paddock and saw that the door of the old shed was open. Sunlight fell through the gaps in the plank walls and lay in dusty strips on the straw that covered the floor. The goat was not there. He looked around carefully. He was not fond of Nina's goat.

He stood on the rocky shelf at the end of the paddock and looked out over the valley to the far slope which was lush and green. It was a view he had come to love. As usual he went over his plan in his mind. A unit, built into the hill so it wasn't obtrusive. With a veranda facing the view. Luxury, of course. Nothing but the best. He imagined himself on his veranda, gin and tonic in hand, as the sun went down behind the hill and the parrots screamed in the valley below his feet. When Nina's holiday camp was up and running, he would suggest it to her. She wouldn't refuse. It would be a payment for all the hard work he'd done on the place.

It was only when he turned away and began walking back up the hill that he heard the singing. It seemed to be coming from beneath his feet. A glorious soaring woman's voice that seemed to melt into the limpid spring sunshine that was almost too hot on the top of his head. A recording, he realised when he heard the orchestra, and then a male voice, thin in comparison and obviously real, singing in unison. For a long moment he stood listening until the song was finished and the music stopped abruptly. Then he watched as someone appeared on the other side of the stone wall, much as Nina had done the first time he had seen her. A lean strong body dressed in old surf gear, much the worse for wear. A dark head, long hair tied back roughly. A young, bearded face. Blue eyes that mirrored his own. John recognised his son with a thud of his heart strong enough to hurt. Relief surged through his body, followed by anger, a more familiar emotion.

'What the hell are you doing here?'

'I live here.'

'How long have you been here?'

'How long since you noticed I was gone?' Michael started ambling up the hill. 'If you're looking for Nina she's not here. She's up at the house.'

'No, hang on a minute.' John reached out and grabbed Michael's arm. 'Do you mean to tell me you're living down there? In the cave?'

Michael shrugged him off. 'There's nothing wrong with living in a cave. We all used to do it once upon a time.'

Swallowing his anger, John nodded towards the cables. 'I see you've made yourself at home.'

'That's only so Nina doesn't have to listen to my music. She's not real keen on opera.' Michael grinned. 'Are you coming up? I'm just on my way to see if Ian's awake.'

'Ian?'

'The baby, Dad. My son.'

'What's he doing here?'

'Collette's working on the computer.'

At the house Michael bounded up the stairs, walked through the kitchen where Nina sat at the table with a telephone clamped to her ear, and disappeared into one of the rooms further up the corridor. He emerged after a little while with a sturdy baby in his arms, pink-faced from sleep.

'*Che gelida manina,*' he sang cheerfully as he walked through the kitchen. 'Your tiny hand is frozen,' he translated for his son, grabbing his little warm paw and shaking it in an attempt to coax a smile from him. The two of them disappeared down the outside stairs.

John sat down at the table and faced Nina.

'Why the hell didn't you tell me he was here?'

Nina hunched her shoulder to hold the phone against her ear and began writing rapidly on a piece of paper. 'He told me not to.'

'Look, Nina …'

'Hang on …' Nina spoke into the phone and hung up. 'Michael told me he didn't want you to know where he was. Simple as that. And why should I tell you anyway? I keep *your* secrets.'

She did, too. She had spoken to Naomi on more than one occasion when she rang Hill End looking for John. They had got quite friendly over the months, chatting about this and that, although never about the thing that Naomi really wanted to know.

'What's he doing living in the cave? There's room in the house, isn't there?'

Nina shrugged. 'His choice. And there's his music, too, see?'

'Yes, so I heard.'

When it came to music, John O'Shea was a middle-of-the-road man. Elton John. Phil Collins. Kate Cerebrano. Anything by Andrew Lloyd Weber. He'd seen Superstar three times when it had been in Brisbane. Not the sort of man to appreciate the rich tones of Cecelia Bartoni negotiating her tonsils around a Rossini aria. Or the rare clear voice of the Romanian soprano, Inessa Galante who was his son's latest passion.

'I don't know why you put up with him, Nina. They're damned dangerous those power cords, you know that, don't you?'

'Oh, leave the boy alone, John, can't you?' The phone rang again. Nina reached to pick it up. 'Put the kettle on, if you've got nothing else to do.'

John got up and wandered over to the sink. He remembered the first cup of tea he'd had in this house. The old black stove by the back door. The little green lemons under the sink. The lamp casting fantastic shadows on the walls. It was not like that any more. There was a microwave oven on the bench next to the sink. A tray with tins of coffee and Milo, and a bag of sugar folded over at the top. A greasy electric frypan connected to the wall by a trailing wire. On the table the remains of a sliced loaf in a plastic bag, a jar of jam with a sticky lid, a mug of gone-cold tea.

The kettle boiled. John made the tea. It was stuffy in the kitchen and Nina's voice went on and on like a fly droning against a window. After a while he got up and went into the little bedroom at the back of the house where he found Collette sitting in front of a computer which was standing

114

on a cluttered desk pushed up against the window. The window was open allowing a little cool air to invade the room. She looked up briefly and smiled. She was wearing glasses with thin wire frames and she pushed them up her nose with one finger.

'Want a cup of tea?' he asked.

She shook her head. 'I'm stopping in a minute.'

'I've seen Michael.'

'Has he got the baby?'

John nodded.

'That's okay then.' She returned to her screen.

John heard the click of the phone and went back into the kitchen.

Nina was sitting at the table with her head in her hands. 'It's times like this I wish I still smoked.' she said. 'Give me something else to think about.'

John took a step forward. Rested his hands palm down on the table. 'I was worried about him, you know, Nina. I even rang his mother in Sydney to see if he was there.'

Nina raised one eyebrow. The mother in Sydney was a new one. She hadn't heard about her before. 'We thought you'd guess where he was. We thought it would be obvious that he was here.'

'I never even thought of it. What's he going to do with himself, Nina? He's dropped out of uni, I suppose you know that.'

'He's helping me. At the moment he is, anyway.'

'Well, that's something, I suppose.'

'And looking after that baby of his while Collette works.'

John shook his head. 'Hardly man's work, is it? Looking after a baby.'

'It was man's work making it, I dare say.'

'Yes, very well. Point taken. But what about his career? I mean, he was going somewhere ...'

'Look, John ...'

Nina reached out her hand but John pulled away. 'Don't say give him time. I've given him plenty of time. And money. And look at him. Living in a cave! Some people you just can't help.' He moved towards the door. 'Want to come for a walk? I'm going over to see how the dormitories are getting on.'

Nina shook her head. 'I haven't got time. Anyway there's not much to see. The bulldozers were in yesterday but they didn't get very far. They said there's too much of a slope and they need a four-wheel drive. More expensive, of course. Just like everything else.'

'Have you thought any more about the cabins I was talking about? I'm still not keen on the dormitory idea'

'It's supposed to be a holiday camp, remember? For families. That was the whole idea. Cheap holidays for those that can't afford them.'

'You'd make more money the other way. There's more than one way of helping kids than giving them a holiday.'

Nina buried her face in her hands. 'Not now, John. Just go, will you? We can talk about it later.'

John walked to the door and then paused and turned around. 'By the way, your goat's not in the paddock.'

Nina groaned. 'Oh, no. Not again. I'll have to get Michael to go and find her. God knows where she'll be this time.'

'What's wrong with her?'

'Spring fever,' said Nina shortly. 'She should be kidding by now but I haven't had a chance to do anything about it.' And then, in response to John's puzzled look. 'She should be pregnant but she isn't.' And then she laughed. 'Don't look so worried. She won't have gone the way you're going. Goats don't like lantana any more than humans do. She'll be on the road to Ney Creek. Running away from home.'

John went down the stairs and under the house. He fetched some rolled-up plans from the back of his car and set out around the front of the house. He followed the churned-up tracks of the bulldozer towards the edge of the paddock. Nina, up from the table to fetch milk from the fridge, glanced out of the window and saw John, plans under one arm, over in the far corner of the front paddock where the lantana grew as big as a house. He was wearing a pair of moleskin trousers and a checked shirt with a button-down collar, and the sight of him, bare-headed in the hazy afternoon sunlight, shook her with a sudden memory. It had been a while ago, whatever it was. But then everything had been a while ago. Peace and quiet and milking the goat had been a while ago. Going to market on a Friday morning had been a while ago. Nowadays she was flat out remembering what day it was, never mind dredging her mind for memories too elusive to be of any importance. She shook her head and went back to the telephone.

Michael sat cross-legged on the sandy floor of the cave with the still-sleepy child sprawled in the hollow made by his legs. In front of him the steep slope of the valley lay in the cool shade of early afternoon. He had changed the music, replacing Rossini with La Bohéme so that he could listen to Rudolpho and Mimi fall in love for what was probably the thousandth time and listen for a certain high note sung by the tenor, which was the closest he had ever come to pure bliss. He re-lit his joint and puffed contentedly. The first half had allowed him to withstand his father's anger for the first time in his life and enjoy the look of impotence in the older man's eyes. Now he would enjoy the second half in peace while his father took his annoyance out on Nina. He smiled to himself at his father's reaction to his choice of living place. Trust him to see it at face value and not to realise that Michael had the pick of Hill End, no contest.

When he had first arrived, he had slept for several nights in what had been Collette's bed. Then, aware of his need for independence - and her own - Nina had shown him the old shed where the children used to sleep. Hidden in the fringe of the forest, it was damp and gloomy, the rows of iron bunks festooned with spiders webs, heavy with dust, the concrete floor cracked and slimy where the rain got in. The following day he discovered the cave when he went down to help Nina clear the shelves of what was left of the yoghurt and cheeses which she was going to keep in one of the newly-arrived fridges.

To begin with he had draped an old curtain across the opening but he seldom found the need to use it. He liked whatever the night offered him - bright moonlight or rain or the thick sprinkle of stars - and his only visitor was a small

117

grey possum with pink ears who came in from time to time in search of scraps of food, tip-toeing across the sandy floor of the cave on tiny clawed feet.

Michael looked down. The child, who seemed to have inherited his mother's love of sleep, had fallen into a doze, his eye-lids fluttering, his breath coming in little grunts and sighs. Michael put his arm around his son, carried him to the bed and laid him down. Then he climbed on next to him and stretched himself out, hands behind his head.

Outside a flock of lorikeets swung noisily along the valley, the sun catching on bright feathers as they flew. But Michael was oblivious to such everyday beauty. He was asleep.

THIRTEEN

Then it was Collette's seventeenth birthday. There were no presents or birthday balloons but only a chilly tea party held in the late afternoon when the sun had already gone from the garden and the beach wind was blowing. Her only guest was a distracted Frank who was painting for an exhibition and needed a supreme effort of will to leave his canvas long enough to sit down with a cup of tea, a sacrifice lost on Collette who was cross to be so ignored.

James was not there. After years of living in Black Rock and commuting to Sydney he had recently made the decision to move there permanently. The fact was the Sydney of the mid-1990s suited James perfectly. It was a place where his eccentricities went unnoticed or were considered part of his charm, something he discovered when he joined a rather arty set inhabiting the edges of Redfern where he was part-owner of a gallery and had a ground floor flat in a renovated biscuit factory.

The gallery had been the first one to show Frank's work and it was not long before James gained a reputation for being able to spot a trend, not an easy thing to do in Sydney where trends come and go with breathless speed or fall by the wayside before anyone has had a chance to pick them up. He painted the brick wall of his courtyard a deep crimson against which he placed a single sculpture from the gallery, lit with a theatre-strength spotlight, took away the curtains and made his dinner parties the talk of the town. He turned the spare bedroom into a make-shift movie theatre which, although it was not a patch on the one at home, still became the place to be on a Friday night when the set came around to eat dinner and watch James' old movies, thus destroying the trade of the new restaurant on the corner which had opened its doors on the strength of their patronage. And he made a lot of money.

The tea shop on the river in Black Rock was leased out to a certain Mrs Muller who had been the convenor of the local school tuck shop until she was kicked out by the salad roll brigade. Her first move was to install a new freezer and a deep-fryer and, by offering half-price kids' meals and thirty five flavours of ice-cream, destroyed the ambience of the place overnight while increasing its profit a hundred times over. So everyone was happy. Except Collette, who missed him.

At the back of the house, the extension remained unfinished. It was unfortunate that Frank's need to paint returned when it did and robbed Collette of any chance of having the new rooms ready before the summer heat arrived. There was a floor, it's true. Walls, yes. Even windows set neatly into their frames. The walls were clad on the outside with fibro chamfers, except for the odds and ends of spaces which Frank had left to be filled with the bits left over at the end of the job. No roof, though. Frank had laid a couple of beams across the space and thrown tarpaulins over the top, fastened down with rope. He didn't want the rain getting in and making the floor swell.

None of the interior walls had been clad and the whole space was a paradise for Ian, just walking, who amused himself by squeezing his little body between the studs and making secret play areas in the corners of the rooms. The junk moved in, as junk always does and Collette, who was used to such things, made no comment but revelled in the dusty, sawdust smell of the rooms and the sound of the tarps flapping in the wind at night which, combined with the roar of the sea beyond the garden, gave her a feeling of security as she lay tucked up in Frank's untidy bed with his long warm body next to hers.

The phone rang. It was a sound Collette was not used to,

even though it rang constantly at her mother's house when she was up there working on the computer.

'I'll get it.' Frank got to his feet and went inside.

He came out moments later with a smile on his face and Ian under his arm.

'I've changed his nappy.' he said, putting the little boy onto unsteady feet.

'Who was it?'

'James. I've been waiting for him to call. He's got your birthday present.' Frank sat down again and held out his cup for a refill. 'Not from him. You'll get that next time he comes up. From me.'

Collette reached out and poured the tea.

'What did you get me?'

Frank stretched out his legs and reached in his shirt pocket for his pouch of tobacco.

'Remember that painting I did last year? The one of your foot? I always liked that one best of all that series. I was sorry I sold it right from the beginning. I asked James to keep a look out for it. See if he could buy it back. And he has. That's what he was ringing about.' He leaned forward, patting his shorts pockets for matches. 'I want you to have it, Collette. As a thank you for being my inspiration.'

'It's worth a lot of money.' Collette had been hoping for something more useful, like a washing machine, about which she had dropped so many hints it was embarrassing,

'Never mind about that. The money's not important. It's your painting. They all were. But that one most of all.' Frank leaned back, puffing blue smoke. And then, 'Where's Ian?'

Ignored by the adults, Ian had taken several tottering steps on the uneven ground, then gone down on his hands and knees and crawled rapidly in the direction of the gap in the hedge that led to the beach. Collette, who had a mother's fine-tuned instinct about how far to allow her child to go before she restrained him, was startled by the panic in Frank's voice and the sudden explosion of movement as he rose from his chair and sprinted across the grass to pick him up.

'He was all right,' she said as Frank dumped her wriggling child on her lap.

'He wasn't all right, Collette. He was nearly out on the beach.'

'He wouldn't have got far.' But Collette could see that Frank was seriously upset. 'You've never liked him going on the beach, have you, Frank? I remember last summer you used to follow us.'

'How do you know that?'

'You have this little cough.' Collette cleared her throat, a dry delicate sound. 'You probably don't even know you're doing it. But I can always tell when you're around. So there you were hiding in the dunes while Ian and I were in the water. I never understood why you didn't just come down and sit on the beach.'

'You know me, Collette. I don't like the beach. I never have.'

'Seems a strange place to live then.'

Frank shook his head. 'It wasn't my choice. It's just where I ended up. And I never thought I'd have to deal with having a child so close to the water.'

Collette wrapped her arms around Ian and leaned forward. 'Is this to do with what happened in Indonesia?'

'What do you know about Indonesia?'

'Only what Jim's told me. That you went there to make a movie. And then you stayed after everyone else went home. That you ruined your career doing it. He said you could have been something really big. That Michael Caine only got his chance because you were sitting on a tropical island on the other side of the world doing fuck all.'

Frank dragged on his smoke. 'Is that what you two talk about when James drives you to Hill End? What else has he told you about me?'

'Not much that I didn't already know. But something happened on that island, didn't it, Frank? That's what Jim says. Only he doesn't know what it was.

'It's none of his business.'

'You can tell me.'

'No, Collette, I can't.'

Collette dropped Ian onto the grass. 'But, Frank, if what happened is going to make you act crazy around Ian, don't you think I ought to know about it?'

The last drag on the cigarette. The butt flicked expertly across the garden. 'It's a long story, Collette. And it happened a long time ago.'

'It doesn't matter then. Don't worry about it.' Collette stood up and began gathering up the remains of their tea.

But Frank said, 'Hold on a minute, Collette.' He reached out one long arm. 'You're right. You do need to know. Come on, leave the dishes and sit down.'

But where to begin? Dredging up memories well hidden for more than twenty years. Pushed to the back of his mind so he didn't have to think about them. Except that they were still there. Still the same. Etched clearly in his mind, as if it had happened yesterday.

To get to the beginning of it you had to go back to a cold November afternoon in the London office of Frank's agent, sitting in the worn leather armchair on the client's side of the big untidy desk drinking sherry and listening to the rain turning to sleet on the window outside. Watching Tony shuffling papers and talking on the telephone. Remember them? The old black bakelite telephones with the brown cloth cords. And that peculiar feeble yellow electric light that was the best those old office buildings could produce especially against the gloom of a winter afternoon. Photos on the wall, crowded cheek by jowl, mostly of people who had disappeared years before but still, they had all been Tony's people. And they had all been somebody once.

And then Tony finished his call, hung up the phone and sat back in his chair, stroking his moustache with the side of one finger. 'How d'you fancy the East Indies?'

'Where's that?' Frank had never heard of it.

'A tropical island, Frank. That's what I'm talking about.' Tony leaned forward and poured sherry carefully into the little glasses. 'It's a comedy adventure. Not your usual stuff, I know. But perhaps it's time to try something different. They asked for you especially.'

Frank didn't take much persuading. He had just finished shooting another one of the historical films that had become his hallmark. Another gang of mediaeval thugs - even at this close distance he was hanged if he could remember who they were - getting up to their usual nasty, murdering tricks. The latest film had been made in one of Wales' draughtier castles - using the real thing was much cheaper than building a set and so authentic - and, just to add to his misery, included two of his least favourite activities, sword fighting and horse riding, at both of which he was spectacularly bad and which took place, on this occasion, on a wide beach in Pembroke with the wind blowing off the Atlantic and his chain mail - knitted out of thick cotton and painted silver - offering no protection whatever from the cold.

In the late 'sixties, the islands of Indonesia were far from the everyday holiday destination they are today. Nobody who travelled there was in any danger of being speared by a surfboard carried by a crazy Australian on a motor bike or of sharing a bus with a gaggle of fresh-permed mid-West widows seeing the world on their late hubbys' hard-earned cash. On the island of Komodo nobody had got around to tethering goats to stakes to feed the dragons. Or building tiers of seats around the feeding ground to accommodate the tourists who came to watch the kill. All that came later. Much later.

Two boats had to be hired to get the gear and the crew onto the island the director had chosen on the advice of a friend of his who fancied himself as a bit of an expert. The island was small, mountainous and covered, for the most part, by thick forest. The only foreign presence was a chap called Jeremy Tomkiss who ran a trading post outside the village, one of thousands of such men scattered like flotsam throughout the east. A big, ginger-haired ex-British Army major with a public school accent and a red nose, he had been left behind when the Second World War retreated, doing some sort of civil servant's job until the empire petered out and then making do with trading copra for the bits and pieces of Western trinkets that the local people found they couldn't live without. He had a native wife and a gaggle of half-grown kids running wild and was happy enough so long as there was something left in the bottom of the whisky bottle.

The local people, not having had enough to do with Westerners to either mistrust them or try to rip them off, were uniformly pleasant, friendly and helpful. The weather was hot. The scenery was spectacular. The beaches were not a bit like Pembroke's cold brown sand but were narrow, gleaming white and fringed with palm trees on one side and sparkling turquoise water on the other. And the women were absolutely gorgeous.

This was what Frank discovered, arriving straight from the gloom of an English February and he found it all very much to his liking. But it was not long before things started to go wrong. For a start the island, though beautiful, was remote and the expense of ferrying in supplies soon had an effect on the film's budget. Fish began to appear on the menu with a regularity that alarmed a group of people who expected a roast dinner on Sunday even when they were living on a tropical island.

Frank's co-star was an up-and-coming comic actress called Carol Morrison who combined a screen presence of considerable charm with a foul-mouthed temper the moment the cameras stopped rolling. She didn't like the island one bit, the lack of an electric socket for her hair drier being the least of her complaints. Then the monsoon came and once the rain began it didn't seem to want to stop and there were days and days when there was no action at all. Time began to run out as actors and crew sat under dripping canvas shelters, playing cards and eating their way through what was left of the money.

Finally the producer decided to cut his losses and write the rain into the script but by then it was too late. With the big love scene yet to come, Frank and Carol were no longer on speaking terms. Carol refused to work in the rain and spent hours leafing through her contract trying to find a clause that said she didn't have to. Half the crew had gone down with dysentery and the rest had made friends with Jeremy and had to be prised away from the whisky bottle every time there was work to be done. In the end the decision was made to call it quits and finish the rest of the film at home in the studios.

But Frank refused to leave.

He had taken up with a native girl, not the only one to do so, not by a long chalk, but Frank didn't believe in doing things by halves and, by the time the crew had packed up and were ready to go, the girl was pregnant and Frank was deeply in love. Far too much in love to think of leaving. And, besides, he had the baby to think of.

'So what did you do?' asked Collette. 'Hide?'

Frank grinned. 'That's what I should have done. No, I just told them my six month contract was up and that was the end of it. They could finish the movie any way they wanted but I wasn't going back to London.'

'Bet they were pleased about that.'

Frank shrugged. 'I didn't care. I just wanted them out of there. In the end they left without me. I think they knew they were beaten. With me or without me, that film was never going to be any good. I don't think it was ever released.'

'Jim said it wasn't.'

'Well, he'd know.'

'So what happened next?'

'Not much. I was living in the village with my girl. Siti, her name was. The men tried to teach me to fish but I wasn't any good at it. I couldn't swim, for a start, and you know what I think of the water. Even beautiful warm tropical water like that didn't tempt me to get wet. Most of the rest of what went on was women's work so there wasn't really anything for me to do. I used to go up and see Jeremy from time to time but we didn't really hit it off. I don't think he was too keen on me living in Siti's village. He said that it was all very well taking one of the local girls, nothing wrong with that so long as you continued to live like a gentleman. Letting the side down, he called it.' Frank laughed shortly. 'There was only him and me on the island, so who was there to care? And, if he thought I wasn't living like a gentleman in that perfect little village sitting on the edge of a tropical island, then he had never lived as I had, growing up in the East End of London with rats in the walls and a cold water tap at the bottom of the yard. And the bombs. I mean, I was being bombed while he was swanning around the east in a staff car telling chaps what to do. His words, them, not mine.'

'And the baby?'

'A boy.' Frank smiled. 'A nice little chap.'

'So you have a son.'

Frank shook his head. 'Not any more.'

'What happened to him?'

'He drowned.'

'Drowned? How?'

'There was a storm. The creek rose. He fell in. He was only four. He didn't really have a chance.

'Did anybody find him?'

'I did.'

It had been the first storm of the season. The village men, reading the signs, had pulled the boats up onto the beach and retreated to the shade to gossip and smoke. Frank had climbed the small headland between the village and Jeremy's place and spent the afternoon on his veranda drinking whisky and watching the clouds building up on the horizon beyond the water.

'We should get something out of it,' observed Jeremy at one stage, mopping his brow, as the afternoon wore on and the humidity increased. 'It's hot enough, damn it.'

After a while they moved inside away from the mosquitoes. Jeremy's wife gave them a meal and, later on, she came into the room with a lamp against the increasing gloom of the afternoon.

The wind came first, hitting the side of the flimsy building like an iron fist and setting the rattan blinds at the windows jumping and banging. Beyond the beach the water roared in a mess of white foam. And then the rain, setting up an urgent drumming on the iron roof over their heads that drowned out the other sounds of the storm. The temperature dropped like a stone. A dog and a small child crept into the room and settled themselves behind the chairs where the two men sat. After a while Jeremy got up and prowled around the house, coming back with a fresh bottle of whisky tucked under one arm while he unscrewed the lid with the other hand.

The storm blew itself out in the early hours of the following morning, leaving behind a mass of debris on the beach and a great brown patch in the water where the creek next to Jeremy's house had emptied itself into the sea. It was mid-morning before Frank was ready to go home. He spent the early part of the day nursing his hangover on the veranda and watching Jeremy working his way slowly around the house fixing up the odd things that had come adrift in the storm. And then, after another bowl of the rice that seemed to be forever on the boil, he set off through the several miles of thick forest that separated Jeremy's house from the village.

There were some trees down along the track and it was hot going with the sun blistering through the remaining moisture in the air and a halo of biting insects to keep him company. The village creek had been up, too. He could see the line of debris showing the extent of the flood and deep gouge marks in the sand where the swift water had carried it away. The water was still high and flowing quickly, full of mud and debris from the forest behind the village.

He was barred from entering his hut. A large woman came stooping out of the doorway as he approached and stood with her arms folded. The woman was Sumiantan, Siti's aunt, a relationship which she seemed to think gave her the right to poke her nose into Frank's affairs, something she did on a regular basis and with an enthusiasm which would have been annoying if it were not for her unfailing good humour and the gap-toothed charm of her smile.

Frank had sufficient of the language by this stage to understand from Sumiantan that his wife was in mourning and was not to be disturbed. The reason for the mourning was that her son was missing, presumed drowned. He had been playing by the creek when the storm started and had fallen in. The men were out looking, said Sumiantan, waving one meaty arm in the direction of the sea, and perhaps Frank might care to look, too, seeing that it was his child who was lost. She gave him a look which was not particularly friendly and which made him feel more of an outsider than he had felt since his arrival in the village five years previously. Small children like Frank's son belonged to the women until they were old enough to sit with the men and learn men's skills so perhaps the feeling of being shut out was not so much because he was a stranger but because he was a man and fit for nothing but searching the mangroves while the women got on with the serious business of mourning,

Frank followed the stream to the beach where the tide was on the ebb, retreating from the narrow stretch of white sand to where the rocks began just offshore. Water from the creek flowed across the beach in sullen brown ribbons to stain the clear water of the pools lying in cracks and crevasses in the shell-encrusted rocks and reflecting a high, pale sky in which the clouds hung like a hazy curtain. He stepped across the rocks, disturbing side-walking crabs and making small fish flicker into shelter.

The tide had gone from the mangroves, leaving a smooth wet slime in which the trees grew thickly, their leaves sweating in the stale heat. Frank skirted the edge of the trees, picking his way through the thick mud and feeling it ooze warm between his toes. The child was lying where the tide had dropped him in the dappled shelter of the first line of trees, on his back in the mud like a grotesque doll. Decay had bloated his body and his skin was stretched over it like an over-stuffed toy. Immersion in the sea had given it a look like smooth leather in which the natural lines and creases of plump childhood appeared like dark cracks. The features of his face were lost in puffy flesh. Only the rust colour of his hair, the thing he had from his father, betrayed his identity. That, and a long white scar on his belly where he had fallen on the rocks several months previously.

Frank bent forward and put out his hands to pick up his child. But this was not his child any more, not any sort of child, this strange child-shaped lump lying on the stinking mud. Underneath the skin there was nothing but empty bones and putrid flesh and the scuttle of crabs disturbed from their feast. Frank crouched in the mud with the remains of his child falling between his fingers and added to the mess with the foul-tasting contents of his stomach. He turned urgently towards the sea, still retching, his hands out in front of him, and waded out until he was in clear water and able to clean himself. Behind him, under the trees, the crabs returned to finish their work

FOURTEEN

There was silence in the garden. Collette sat on the edge of her chair, hunched over, her arms tight around her body, hanging on for dear life. She reached down to where Ian was sitting next to her chair chewing on a dry leaf and pulled him onto her lap.

Frank sighed deeply. 'So now do you see why I've always kept such a close eye on Ian? I'm terrified something is going to happen to him. I don't know how I'm going to cope when he's old enough to run around.'

'We don't have to stay here, Frank. We can go and live somewhere else, if we want to.' Collette stood up and handed the baby to Frank while she began to gather the dishes.

'So we can.' Frank got to his feet, slinging the baby under one arm. 'I'm going in. This little chap needs his bath.'

'So what did you do? After you found your little boy in the mangroves.' Collette was sitting at the kitchen table spooning mashed vegetables into Ian's mouth.

Frank got up to attend to the chops and potatoes spluttering in the frying pan. 'What did I do? I ran. That's what I did.' He turned to get the knives and forks out of the drawer. 'Back over the hill to Jeremy's place. There was a boat in, one of the local vessels that traded between the islands. I knew the crew, local lads mostly, and I asked them to give me a lift when they left the island in the morning.'

He opened a can of beans and dumped them into a saucepan. 'We were a couple of weeks island-hopping before we got somewhere big enough to give me a chance to get a ride out. I got a berth on a rusty old tub that was going to Jakarta. I was hired as the cook, which was a bit of a joke. I mean, I was a film star, right?'

He stirred the beans rapidly, peering into the pan. 'From Jakarta I was taken on a vessel sailing to Australia. A funny set up that was, too. Portuguese captain, Philippino crew, and me. Armed to the teeth against pirates. Or so they said. I never did find out what they were carrying. But the captain liked a drink and so did I and I kept him amused with yarns about the movies though I don't think he believed half of what I told him.'

Frank put the plates of food on the table and sat down. 'Melbourne was the first port of call. A cold, miserable autumn day. Drizzling rain. I got myself a room in a boarding house and a bottle of whisky and crawled into bed. The next day I took myself into town to buy some clothes and find out what was going on. I remember drinking coffee in Collins Street and watching the trams go by. The sun was out and I can tell you a warm watery Melbourne sun on a cool day can feel pretty good. Especially when you are a young bloke, decked out in good gear and just about to take the place by storm.'

Frank took a bite of food and chewed thoughtfully, watching Collette take Ian out of the highchair and settle herself down in the chair by the fire while the baby hunted sleepily for her breast.

'And did you?'

Frank shook his head. 'It wasn't as easy as I thought. Oh, I did the rounds of the agents. Sat at desks in shoddy rooms and told my story. And they'd all heard of me. Even in Melbourne, even in those days, they'd heard of me. But what they knew wasn't particularly encouraging. A trouble-maker. That's what I was. Unreliable. And they wouldn't touch me with a barge-pole.

In the end I met a bloke in a pub who told me that one of the commercial TV stations was planning a new detective series and they were looking for someone to play the lead role. I'd never really considered doing television but, by then, I was getting desperate. Of course, they jumped at it. I mean, I could act. There was no problem about that. And

I had the look they were after. Originally this detective was supposed to be an Italian - you know, dark-skinned and a bit seedy looking - but, when I came along, they changed it to a gone-off-the-rails Englishman. That was the whole point, you see, that this chap had just about had it, was always just about to lose his job, but he always got his man and he always managed to survive until the next show.

It became a very popular series. Ran for eight years. And it was me people wanted to see. I was the star and they knew it, too, the producers and the channel bosses, no matter how hard they wanted to get rid of me. Because I made it hard for them. I really did. Unreliable wasn't the word for it. I was drunk, see? Drunk the whole time.'

Frank finished his meal and pushed his plate away. Got up and filled the kettle at the sink. 'I remember we used to do the outdoor stuff once a month. It was kept to a minimum because it cost money but out we'd go into the wilds of suburbia and pretend to shoot each other from behind parked cars. There wasn't any money in the budget for car chases or any of that sort of thing. You'd never get away with it these days on a top rating police drama like Darbyshire was at the time. People want to see things being blown up. I've never worked out exactly why.

We used to go to a different suburb every week because people liked to play spot the street. It was another reason they watched the show. Television was new enough in those days for it to be a thrill to see something familiar on the box. Afterwards we'd go to the nearest pub for a few drinks. The crew used to leave my address with the barman, plus the price of a ride home, and I'd get poured into a cab at ten o'clock and sent home to bed. There are plenty of taxi drivers in Melbourne who've put Frank Duncan to bed, I can tell you.'

'So where did Patsy come in?' Collette heaved the sleeping child onto her shoulder where he hung, slack-faced, his eyes half shut.

'Patsy? She was part of the deal.' Frank lifted the boiling kettle from the stove and made the tea. 'They told me to get myself a wife. The women's magazines preferred their celebrities to be married and the bosses liked to see my face on the cover of as many magazines as possible. I met Patsy at a party. She was doing some sort of publicity work for one of those glossy magazines that nobody ever reads. Being Patsy Duncan suited her down to the ground. Plenty of money. Plenty of glamour. And it was one in the eye for her father. She came from an old Melbourne family, see? A TV detective was hardly their idea of a good catch for their daughter. Mind you, I think her father was quite pleased when Patsy changed her name to Duncan. He was getting tired of her dragging his name through the mud.'

'Why? What did she do?'

'Boys. Drugs. Wild parties. Driving around in sports cars and crashing into things. The usual sort of stuff. But I liked Patsy's dad, I really did. And her mother thought the world of me. Don't ask me why. So it wasn't as bad as it could have been. And she did her job. Got her face in more magazines than I've had hot dinners. But you know what, Collette? I can't remember eating a meal with her. Not one. I suppose I must have. We were together for eight years. But I can't remember any of them.' He came around the table and lifted the sleeping child from her shoulder. 'You eat your dinner. I'll go and pop him into bed.'

'It's strange,' he said, coming back into the room. 'All those years. All those long years. And all of a sudden they're gone. And here I am'

'I don't know what you mean.'

'It's just such a strange feeling to look back over all those years and realise I don't have to think about them any more. It doesn't matter who I was or what I did. Not now'

'It wasn't your fault. That little boy.'

'I know. But I ran. That's the thing I think about.'

'Sometimes running is the only thing you can do.' Remembering how she'd run from Hill End.

'I spoke to a forensic scientist once. We used to get all sorts of experts on the show, helping us with the scripts. He said I was unlucky to find him. A few minutes earlier and he would have been out at sea. A couple of hours later and the tide would have taken him away. What was left of him. It was the heat that did for my little chap. The hot weather plus the fact he had been in the water the whole time. And those damned crabs.' Frank shuddered. 'I hate the things. This bloke told me to forget about it and try to remember the child as he had been. But I can't remember a thing about him except seeing him the day he was born, all slimy and bloody and bawling his head off, and that bit in the mangroves.'

Collette stood up and put her arms around his neck. 'Poor Frank.'

'No, it's gone now.' Frank linked his hands behind her waist and rested his face on top of her head. 'Gone a while ago, I think.' He put his hands on her shoulders and pushed her away then lowered his head to look into her eyes. 'I'm going to Venice in a couple of months. Do you want to come?'

'Venice?'

'European city? Where the gondolas come from?'

'Frank! I'm not that dumb. Yes, I'll come. Of course I will.'

'Just like that? It's a long way, Collette. And you've never flown before.'

'Neither have you.'

'I flew from London to Indonesia. Three days all up. It was a long way in those days.'

'Yeah, in those days. How long ago was that?'

Frank grinned. 'What a very aggressive little person you are all of a sudden.'

'You haven't told me why we're going yet.'

'Oh, there's a festival on. James managed to get a couple of my pictures accepted for an exhibition of Australian contemporary art. It was his idea for you to go. He thought you might like it.'

Collette smiled. 'I don't know why Jim likes me so much.'

'Because you're a pet, that's why.' Frank kissed her briefly on her forehead. 'I'm off out for a breath of air. Do you want to come?'

But Collette could never see the point of walking on the beach at night especially with the wind working itself up to a gale and, after Frank had gone, she sat down in the old armchair by the fire, nursing her cup of tea and listening to the cat purring sleepily from the back of the chair and the wind buffeting the house, and thought about her painting.

Collette's foot so sweet and white resting on the seabed with the sunlight falling through the water and the little fishes nibbling delicately on her flesh. She'd never liked that painting. Now she knew why.

FIFTEEN

It was a day in late November when Nina finally realised what she had done. Two weeks until the official opening and with bookings coming in for camp sites and cabins, she lifted her head up from her lists and, realising that it was lunch-time, wondered if Michael was close enough to call in for a sandwich. He had been out at the pool site all morning, planting trees he said, although she was at a loss to understand why he needed to make such a noise doing it.

All morning she had listened to the sound of people shouting and the rumble of machinery. But noise had been her constant companion for the last four or five weeks ever since she had argued with John O'Shea about the need for a pool and lost, not only that they should have one at all but that it should be a decent size and properly done. She had conceded the need for some sort of water to swim in but had planned a rock pool, a widening of the creek where it meandered through the trees on the far side of the property. Something everyone could use. Picnickers, as well as guests.

But John had started quoting laws at her. How she could be made liable for any accidents that might happen in a rock pool that she had created and not fenced or had patrolled by a registered lifeguard. How even trespassers could sue landowners for injury and get away with a decent pay-out without any difficulty at all. He was very good at that, John, always ready with the wet blanket just when Nina felt she was getting on top of things. Although it seemed to her that the whole project had slipped out of her control very quickly, in fact almost as soon as she had expressed the idea that, if she had to use her capital for something, as John insisted she must, she might like to have people come to Hill End for their holidays. After all, the whole idea – Cliff's idea - of Hill End was that it should be shared with other people and perhaps that was what he had intended she should do with the money when he left it to her in his will. But her idea of doing up the old bunkhouse and offering it to church groups and welfare organisations was doomed as soon as it was voiced. It seemed that the whole project was hedged about with so much legislation that it was impossible to do something as simple as invite people to stay. Danger lurked around every corner, accidents waiting to happen and, behind every accident, a lawyer rubbing his hands in glee so that Nina began to wonder how anybody managed to negotiate life at all without regular appearances in a court of law.

And so everything had to be done properly and, after a while, John began to express the opinion that it was a pity to waste such a nice development on the needy and perhaps it would be a better idea to turn Hill End into a money-making venture and simply donate to charitable causes rather than having the objects of charity turning up to stay. It was not an opinion that Nina shared although the idea that people might have to pay to stay at Hill End, never a consideration when the idea was first mooted, became more and more of a possibility as Nina began to realise not only how much the whole project had cost to build but how much it was going to cost to run on a day to day basis. John had spent a whole morning discussing the important matter of cash flow, another new concept for Nina for whom cash had never been more than an occasional luxury, and had followed the discussion with a pub lunch in Ney Creek and an offer of a generous slug of money just to tide her over for the first six months of trading. Nina said she would think about it.

She didn't much care for John's assumption that he was somehow part of the Hill End project, even though she admitted to herself that she would have been lost without his help and advice over the past few months, and she was even less pleased when he told her, somewhat hesitantly, of his plan to build himself a luxury unit on the slope behind the house. Of course, it had to be there, didn't it? Where the cave was. The best place on the whole property. Many a time she and Cliff had slept there together on soft summer nights and woken when the sun touched the tip of the mountain and filled the valley with golden fire. It had paintings in it too, that cave, although they were hard enough to see if you didn't know they were there. Not so easy to see at the moment, certainly, with the majority of them covered by Michael's surf posters, stuck up with blu-tac. She'd known about the painting for years, having been told about them by old Ed who used to busk his didgeridoo at the Ney Creek markets. According to the old man, the cave had been used for thousands of years by his tribe on its circuit from coast to forest and was only abandoned when the white man settled the land and forced them out. He said, too, that the cave protected its own and told her to use it carefully or accept the consequences. Not that Nina had taken much notice. Hadn't she used it for years to keep her yoghurts and cheeses cool? And nothing had ever happened to her.

However, she told John bluntly that the cave was a sacred site and couldn't be touched. And he said, of course, he had the utmost respect for the rights of the indigenous population, while his mind was busy with the idea of a screen of non-reflective glass covering the paintings and the whole wall incorporated into his living room. In fact, the more he thought about it, the more he liked it and the more inclined he was to give more serious thought to the idea of moving to Hill End permanently. He could install the latest technology so that he could work from home and go up to Brisbane only when he had to appear in court. Offer Collette a job. She seemed to know her way around computers and that sort of thing. The idea was very attractive. And, if Naomi didn't like it, then that would be tough luck.

But Nina had gone home from lunch with her head full of misgivings, a mood not improved by the sight of a bright yellow industrial sized back-hoe chewing great lumps out of the front paddock and loading them onto a truck.

Now Nina walked through the house and onto the veranda and found out quickly enough the source of the noise that had been teasing her ears all morning. There was a truck standing near the pool loaded with several large palm trees, their roots tied up in canvas bags. Several more of these large trees had been planted already and stood, leaning somewhat drunkenly in their holes, looking quite ridiculous against the backdrop of dry, stony paddocks. There was a crane on the truck and a tree lashed to the crane, its trunk protected with more of the brown hessian that covered its roots. There was a considerable amount of shouting as the crane began lifting the tree into the air and moving it slowly in the direction of a large hole in the ground. Michael looked up and saw Nina watching and began walking towards the house, shouting instructions over his shoulder to the men left behind. Half way to the house he turned around and walked backwards, watching the scene at the pool with obvious satisfaction. The palm tree, hanging in mid-air, turned around slowly on the end of its chain. Nina turned away and went back into the house.

'Cheese and onion all right for you?' she said when Michael came into the kitchen 'It's that or nothing. I haven't had a chance to go to the shops.'

Michael opened the fridge door and stared inside gloomily. 'No tomatoes?'

'They're all finished.' Nina sawed at the bread, cutting it into untidy chunks. She put a couple of pieces on a plate and handed them across the table. 'Help yourself to cheese.'

'I'll take you to the shops this afternoon, if you like. Soon as I've finished outside.'

'Look, Michael ...' Nina buried her face in her hands and rubbed her eyes with her fingers. 'Send them away. Those men ...' She gestured with her head. 'Tell them I've changed my mind.'

'Changed your mind? About the trees? What's wrong with them? Nina, what's wrong? You're not crying, are you?'

Up came her head. 'If I'm not I should be. Look what we've done, Michael. Look what I've done.'

'What?'

'The whole thing.' Her arms swept a great circle in the air. 'All of it. That swimming pool. The cabins. Showers and toilets. Trees cut down so the power could come in. Fences to keep people out. What d'you think Cliff would say if he could see it? Eh?'

Michael shook his head. 'I don't know.'

'This isn't what he wanted. He'd have a fit if he could see what I've done. And it isn't what I want either.'

'But I thought it was what you decided to do. You and my father.'

'Your father! He should have left me alone. I was better off the way I was.'

Michael sighed. Filled his bread with cheese. Took a large bite. Chewed. 'So what now?'

'Take me to Ney Creek after lunch. I want to buy a straw of semen.'

'A what?'

'A straw of semen. To impregnate the goat. It's long overdue. A box of day-old chicks, too, if there are any to be had. Although I should have a look at the chook-house first.'

'But what about the rest of it? The pool ...'

'Fill it in. I don't want it.'

'But Nina ...'

'Look, Michael. Don't pester me, okay? At the moment all I know is what I don't want. There'll be plenty to time to work things out later. When I've had a chance to think.'

Michael finished his sandwich. 'What I can't understand is what made you decide on this holiday resort idea in the first place.'

'Shit, Michael, I don't know.' She shrugged. 'It seemed like a good idea at the time.'

But Michael persisted. 'I thought the idea of Hill End was more about what you had before. When I first came here. You and the goat and the vege patch. Nobody telling you what to do. I thought it was paradise.'

'Well, it was. I just thought Cliff would want me to share it, that's all.'

'But you did share it, Nina. You shared it with me.'

There was silence for a long moment. Then, 'I suppose I did. I hadn't thought of it like that before. And you think that's enough?'

'What if ...' Michael laid his knife very carefully on the table. 'What if Cliff left you the money so you could be free. Nothing more than that. Free to do what you like. He knew the place needed money to keep it going. Like the rates. Like the rego on the ute. Which I have paid, by the way. It was three years out of date! But not to do anything fancy with it. Just to have it so you could live the way you want. The way you did when he was alive.'

'Let the money stay in the bank for when I need it?'

'Yes, why not?'

'John – your father – said I should use it. He said it was a crime to leave money lying idle.'

'He spends a lot of time down here,' said Michael thoughtfully. 'I wonder what he wants? Apart from fucking you.'

Nina flinched. 'I seem to remember it was something of the sort between you and my daughter that brought your father down here in the first place.'

'Yes, but that was only to pay the rates and he did that on day one. No need for all this.' Michael picked up his knife and cut another hunk from the cheese. 'You know what I reckon? I reckon he's after a piece of the action.'

'A piece of what action?'

'Part of this bloody holiday camp thing we've been building.'

'What makes you think that?'

'He'd be mad if he didn't. It's going to make money, you know. Whether you want it to or not.'

'He offered me money the last time he was here. Said I'd need it to tide me over.'

'Did you take it?'

Nina shook her head. 'I told him I'd think about it. He said he wanted to build himself a house. Down by the cave.'

'Ah, shit,' said Michael quietly. 'The cave, eh? I might have known. The fuckin' bastard.' And then, 'You're not in love with him or anything, are you, Nina?'

Nina shook her head. 'No danger of that.'

Suddenly there swam into her mind an image of John O'Shea, plans under one arm, walking in the sunshine towards the lantana patch where now stood the new cabins. She remembered how the sight of him had stirred something in her memory, something she hadn't taken the trouble to locate. Now she knew what it was. Three men. Walking in the same place. Rolled up plans under their arms.

'Michael, do you know what would have happened to this place if you father hadn't paid the rates?'

'It was going to be sold to a mob of developers, wasn't it? That's what Collette said. They were going to turn it into some sort of resort.'

'A holiday resort. That's what Hill End was going to be. Look around you, Michael. It's happened. And you know the worst thing about it? We did it. You and me. Working for your fucking father.'

Michael tipped back his head and howled with laughter, which brought the old dog hurrying from her sleeping spot at the top of the stairs to crouch by his chair and stare up at him with puzzled eyes.

'I don't know what you find so funny,' said Nina crossly.

'Oh, come on, Nina, you've got to laugh. The old bastard!' Michael leaned forward. 'Look, Nina, it isn't Cliff's money any more. And it isn't my fucking father's either. It's yours. So just do what you like with it, that's what I say. Now, come on, and I'll take you into town.'

Nina stood up. 'Just let me clear the table. You go and tell those blokes to stop planting trees, will you, Michael? I'll pick you up at the gate.'

Nina drove the ute to the gate where Michael was waiting. She slid across the seat so he could get in behind the steering wheel. He looked across at her and grinned. 'I told them they could do what they liked with the trees,' he said, nodding with his head in the direction of the men grouped around the truck. 'There'll be a few big trees in little yards by tonight I reckon.'

'Good luck to them.'

Nina leaned her head against the back of the seat and closed her eyes, feeling the car surge beneath her as Michael attacked the narrow mountain road. He'd put a couple of concrete blocks in the back of the ute to improve its cornering and was testing their effect as the vehicle took the steep curves leading down to the creek. He narrowed his eyes against the sun and sat forward a little watching the road as the car took the corner at the beginning of the long slope down to the creek.

The ute went down the slope a little sideways and crossed the narrow log bridge too fast, making the loose planks jump and creak. On the other side he took one hand off the wheel to wave to Mr Jackson, the bus driver, who was negotiating the school bus with ponderous care down the opposite slope. He left the bus rocking in his wake as he accelerated the ute up the slope, its rear end hopping on the uneven surface of the road. Michael felt the concrete blocks begin to slide and he twitched the steering wheel so that the back wheel bit the dirt on the side of the road, spitting gravel. He glanced across the cabin and there was Nina smiling, her arms above her head, a posture he recognised from Collette.

'What's up with you?'

'I'm having a good time. Nothing wrong with that, is there?'

The stock agent was on the far side of town and Michael took the car through the streets at a more sedate pace and parked it by the pub, nose in to the kerb. He was sitting on the veranda in front of his second cold beer when Nina returned, stepping daintily across the dusty street with her purse under one arm and a small blue coolite container dangling by a string handle from her hand.

'Chickens on Friday,' she announced, sitting down opposite him. 'Give you time to get the chook house fixed up. Hurry up, Michael. This stuff doesn't last for ever.'

'Finish this, then.' He pushed his beer glass across the table.

She drank. 'You're not going anywhere, are you?'

'Taking you home, I thought.'

'No, I mean leaving Hill End. I think I'd miss you if you weren't around.'

Michael shrugged. 'I've got nowhere else to go.' He stood up, banging his pockets for the keys. 'Anyway you'll have more than just me to keep you company soon enough. I'm looking after Ian for a few weeks. Collette's going to Venice.'

'Venice? Collette is? Lucky girl! And we get to have Ian.'

'Good, eh?'

But whether he meant Venice, or Ian, Nina had no idea.

SIXTEEN

An early summer morning. Baby on hip, Collette opens her front door and waves to the driver of the big black car waiting at the front gate. 'Frank! The car's here!'

Four year old Ian, in aeroplane-patterned pyjamas, scuttles past her and runs down the path. The driver gets out of the car and walks around to the passenger side. He opens the door with due ceremony and the little boy climbs in.

Finally Frank arrives, face damp from shaving, tugging a comb through his hair. He kisses Collette and the baby, walks to the car, tickles Ian until he squeals, then watches the child run back up the path to his mother. Majestically the car moves away from the footpath and enters the stream of traffic.

Collette is no longer in Black Rock but in Brisbane, sharing a house with Frank and her two little boys, Ian and baby Max who was conceived during their trip to Venice. The house is near the railway line at Indooroopilly, a big old Queenslander with original coloured glass panels in the windows and fretwork over the doors, the sort of old house where the dust falls invisible from walls and windows and lies like a ghost on every surface, despite Collette's best efforts to chase it off.

Frank is making a movie. A made-for-television political thriller about the Australian Labor Party and the CIA, a tale with more than a grain of truth in it and one which is set to ruffle the odd feather or two on its release. For Frank an otherwise excellent project is marred only by the fact that it is based in the 1970s which means he has to wear flared trousers and tight body shirts with long collars, something which made Collette snigger until he pointed out that at least he hadn't been born in that inelegant era, as she had been.

Collette is enjoying the pace of life in the city, even though James tells her that it is a snail's pace, compared with Sydney. Of course, James is thrilled to bits that his old friend is back in the movie industry and visits Brisbane regularly in the hope that some of Frank's fame might rub off on him: well enough deserved, he thinks, after the number of times he heaved him out of pubs.

Leaving the little boys with a uni student baby sitter, Frank, James and Collette trawl the pub and coffee house scene in Paddington and West End watching live bands and listening to poetry, an odd looking trio in the crowd of students, new-agers and wanna-be office workers looking for a bit of action after a day in the air-conditioning. James sleeps in the spare room at the back of Collette's house, listening to the trains echoing in the quiet night and wakes to the sound of early-rising children, thumping and crashing in the next room.

The picture of Collette's foot hangs over the bed she shares with Frank but now it reminds her not of Frank's long-dead son but of their trip to Venice and of that strange attic room with the leaky roof where his pictures had been hung for the ten days of the festival.

Frank and Collette arrived in Venice at the tail-end of a cold, wet February. To begin with, the weather horrified Collette and she refused to leave their hotel room, spending her time watching in amazement as the tide crept in over the wide tiled plaza outside her window. Venetians and tourists alike hurried along narrow wooden duckboards, their faces hunched into their collars, ignoring the wrought-iron chairs and tables knee-deep in brown flood water where a few hours later they would sit drinking coffee in fitful sunshine as if the tide had never been and would not be again before the end of the day.

Finally Frank persuaded her to come to the gallery where she climbed the marble stairs in the narrow, musty building, which had been the palace of some long-dead duke, to the very top where there was a long gallery topped with a leaky glass skylight. The walls had been painted white and hung with paintings, six of which were Frank's. There was a crew of cheerful Australians who spent their days handing out leaflets, trying to get the spotlights working and complaining unsuccessfully about the leak. After all, what were a few drops of water to a people who lived in a city that leaked like a sieve?

A photographer managed to persuade Collette to pose in front of her painting which didn't need a spotlight to show off its charms, hanging as it was under the shifting grey light created by the rain falling on the skylight. The photograph made its way eventually into the Arts section of the Weekend Australian, much to the delight of James Curtis back home in Sydney who cut it out with tender care and put it aside to show Collette on her return.

The exhibition's budget which had seemed perfectly reasonable in Canberra proved totally inadequate in a city as expensive as Venice. Having spent a small fortune on the spotlights which never did anything apart from the odd alarming flicker, the crew found themselves with little money left over for the non-essentials like food. But Frank entertained the waiters in the hotel's restaurant with some extremely old-fashioned Italian, dredged up from a movie he'd made before any of them were born, and found himself with an invitation to eat with them one evening after the restaurant closed.

Close on midnight he and Collette sloshed across the piazza and followed the restaurant staff down several narrow side streets until they ducked through a doorway and found themselves in a roaring, light-filled room thick with the aroma of red wine and garlic. That they were Australians made them instant friends in a crowd where everyone seemed to have relatives in Sydney or Melbourne. The mention of several suburbs in those cities gave them celebrity status, a small stained table near to the fire, and a supply of wine that only ran out when they staggered into the wind-driven rain sometime after three o'clock the following morning.

From then on the Australian crew ate well every evening. The food was cheap and plentiful, the wine given freely on the promise that they would look up this uncle or that cousin on their return to Australia.

By day Collette explored the city sometimes alone, sometimes in the company of one or two of the crew, Frank being permanently occupied with seminars and master classes, the reason for the all-expenses-paid trip. She visited dress shops and jewellers. She learned to drink espresso coffee without sugar. She bought chocolate which she and Frank ate in bed on the nights when they got there at all. The churches and palaces she left well alone, preferring shops full of new things to fusty old buildings full of dull paintings.

When the ten days were over they travelled by train to Lake Como where the sun was shining on the last of the snow. Frank took Collette into a shop and bought her a set of exquisite silk underwear in palest blue trimmed with Swiss lace. Collette was wearing this underwear on the day she and Frank were married in James' back-yard on a hot March day a week after their arrival back in Australia. As well as negotiating a lucrative contract for Frank's designs on an exclusive line of household linen, James had arranged Frank's divorce from Patsy, a curiously anticlimactic and civilised affair when compared with the years of their marriage. Patsy knew when she was beaten and a generous settlement made the loss of her famous husband so much easier to accept.

James draped his red wall with white muslin and bought two large orange trees in full bloom planted in enormous terracotta pots. He was disappointed that Collette chose to be married, not in white muslin to match his wall, but in a plain linen dress although she did consent to wear a small wreath of flowers on her hair, which was still showing the style of the Venetian hairdresser who had bemoaned its disarray in mournful and unintelligible Italian for the whole hour it had taken for him to cut it.

The whole day showed signs of James' flair and good taste but it was not really what Collette would have chosen for herself. The food was superb, the wines carefully selected, the guests hand-picked and uniformly good-natured. But Collette, who was still queasy from the long flight and not interested in talking to strangers however cheerful they may be, spent the afternoon twisting her new gold ring around and around her finger and longing to go home to Ian.

Not long after Collette's trip to Europe Nina and Michael moved to a new brick house on ten acres of rich river country near Beenleigh where Nina began breeding goats. Once she got over her disappointment that Nancy would never be a champion nor the mother of one she began to do well. Her goats have won ribbons at the Beenleigh Show, and at Ipswich, and she has hopes for next year's Brisbane Exhibition where the winning of a ribbon would mark her arrival in the close-knit world of goat people.

Michael does the general work around the property and drives the ute, now permanently loaded with hay or bags of feed so that it corners beautifully. With his skin burnt black by the sun and his body lean from hard work, he is better looking than ever, a fact not lost on the local girls spotting him in town loading bags into the back of the ute or following Nina around the supermarket. However, Michael is not interested and the girls, annoyed by his indifference, decide that he must be Nina's toyboy. Or a queer. Of course, neither is true. Michael's interests lie elsewhere. In the farm. In Nina's money, which he manages with a mixture of caution and flair that would have made his father proud if he'd known anything about it. In his precious music and his regular Friday night spot on Brisbane's volunteer FM radio station. And in his son.

He sees Ian every week when he goes to Brisbane to do his radio, and once a month he takes the little boy back to the farm. The two of them go off on the motor bike across the paddocks to fish in the river, or stroll through the sheds to see the goats in their white-painted stalls. Or visit the garden to hunt for ripe tomatoes or to gather a handful of beans for dinner, always with a weather eye open for the geese which had frightened Ian once by hissing and pecking at his legs. And then at night eating an early dinner with the little boy, already bathed and ready for bed, sitting up on a cushion with a tea-towel tucked into the neck of his pyjamas and his favourite food to eat, cooked by a doting grandmother. Occasionally Michael sees his father's picture in the paper or hears his name mentioned on the radio and pities him although John O'Shea, who has put the whole sorry saga to the back of his mind, is unaware of his son's pity or the reason for it.

And Hill End itself?

Nina sold it to a Sydney property developer with a heart condition who had been told by his doctor to slow down. He was happy to pay top dollar for Hill End where everything was already done and only needed his magic touch to make it a success. He was looking forward to a guest list of jaded businessmen in need of a break and planned a gymnasium with a big heated spa and glass walls overlooking the valley. He lasted six months and, after the funeral, his widow packed her bags and moved to a penthouse apartment on the Gold Coast which was what she'd wanted to do in the first place.

And Hill End went back to the forest. A season of heavy rain sent the weeds in the front paddock racing towards the skies, followed by the thick, scrubby growth of wattle and casuarina. A branch from the old mango tree crashed onto the goat shed roof during a storm and remained tangled in the wreckage of split timber and corrugated iron, blocking the path to the cave where Michael's posters faded and curled and fell to the floor, leaving the ancient paintings gleaming in the half-light filtered by a curtain of vines that hid the door. Mats of green weeds covered the surface of the swimming pool where frogs croaked on warm summer nights and laid their eggs in the filter boxes where the water was cool and still.

These days there is little to see from the road but thick green growth and the dilapidated timbers of the gate upon which a faded For Sale sign flutters in the breeze created by the school bus as it ferries a new batch of kids down to the high school in Ney Creek.

www.ingramcontent.com/pod-product-compliance
Lightning Source LLC
Chambersburg PA
CBHW070044260626
47159CB00005B/2123

* 9 7 8 0 9 5 8 0 4 8 9 6 5 *